the twilight

breaking dawn

— part 1 —

THE OFFICIAL ILLUSTRATED MOVIE COMPANION

BY MARK COTTA VAZ

LITTLE, BROWN AND COMPANY
NEW YORK BOSTON

Little, Brown and Company

Hachette Book Group
237 Park Avenue, New York, NY 10017
Visit our website at www.lb-teens.com

Little, Brown and Company is a division of Hachette Book Group, Inc.
The Little, Brown name and logo are trademarks of Hachette Book Group, Inc.

The Twilight Saga: Breaking Dawn name, logo, and related motion picture marks; and the
Summit Entertainment name and logo are trademarks of Summit Entertainment, LLC.

Academy Award® is the registered trademark and service mark of
the Academy of Motion Picture Arts and Sciences.

The publisher is not responsible for websites (or their content)
that are not owned by the publisher.

First Edition: December 2011

Book design by Georgia Rucker Design
All photographs by Andrew Cooper unless otherwise credited

ISBN 978-0-316-13411-8

10 9 8 7 6 5 4 3 2 1

WOR

PRINTED IN THE UNITED STATES OF AMERICA

To Stephenie Meyer, Bill Condon, Wyck Godfrey, and the cast and crew
who are bringing *The Twilight Saga* to its conclusion;
and to my mother, Bettylu Sullivan Vaz, for . . . well, *everything*!

—M.C.V.

Making movie magic is hard work, particularly for a production as
anticipated as *The Twilight Saga: Breaking Dawn Part 1*. It takes a talented
team on both sides of the camera. The following artists, superstars in their
disciplines, graciously spoke about their creative journey:

BILL CONDON, DIRECTOR

MELISSA ROSENBERG, SCREENWRITER

VIRGINIA KATZ, FILM EDITOR

GUILLERMO NAVARRO, DIRECTOR OF PHOTOGRAPHY

RICHARD SHERMAN, PRODUCTION DESIGNER

LORIN FLEMMING, ART DIRECTOR

MICHAEL WILKINSON, COSTUME DESIGNER

DAVID SCHLESINGER, SET DECORATOR

JAN BLACKIE-GOODINE, SET DECORATOR

JOHN BRUNO, VISUAL EFFECTS SUPERVISOR

JEAN BLACK, MAKEUP DEPARTMENT HEAD

RITA PARILLO, ASSISTANT HAIR DEPARTMENT HEAD

PENG ZHANG, CO-FIGHT COORDINATOR

SCOTT ATEAH, STUNT COORDINATOR

JOHN ROSENGRANT, ANIMATRONIC AND SPECIAL MAKEUP EFFECTS
SUPERVISOR, LEGACY EFFECTS

TIPPETT STUDIO, *BREAKING DAWN* TEAM

PHIL TIPPETT, VISUAL EFFECTS SUPERVISOR

ERIC LEVEN, VISUAL EFFECTS SUPERVISOR

KEN KOKKA, VISUAL EFFECTS PRODUCER

NATE FREDENBURG, ART DIRECTOR

TOM GIBBONS, ANIMATION SUPERVISOR

MIKE CAVANAUGH, EDITOR

WYCK GODFREY, PRODUCER

BILL BANNERMAN, CO-PRODUCER AND AERIAL UNIT DIRECTOR

I wanted the complete experience before I traded in my warm, breakable, pheromone-riddled body for something beautiful, strong . . . and unknown. I wanted a *real* honeymoon with Edward. And, despite the danger he feared this would put me in, he'd agreed to try.[1]

Robert Pattinson as Edward Cullen and Kristen Stewart as Bella Cullen, on their honeymoon.

TABLE OF CONTENTS

INTRODUCTION:
THE LAST CHAPTERS

I peeked up at him one more time, and regretted it.
He was glaring down at me again, his black eyes
full of revulsion. As I flinched away from him,
shrinking against my chair, the phrase *if looks
could kill* suddenly ran through my mind.[2]

It was wonder at first sight. Isabella "Bella" Marie Swan, a shy girl freshly transplanted from arid Phoenix, was having lunch on her first day at Forks High School in rainy Washington state. She found herself entranced by five "inhumanly beautiful" students lounging at the farthest table in the cafeteria. They looked like airbrushed fashion-magazine cover models and appeared to be as sun-deprived as the Olympic rain-forest region itself, their strange pallor offset by eyes ringed with shadows, as if they were fatigued from sleepless nights. Bella was particularly drawn to "the beautiful boy" whose dark eyes suddenly met hers. They exchanged furtive glances until lunchtime ended and Bella had to get to Biology II class. Fate seated her next to the beautiful boy,

but suddenly her glances met eyes of fury. She wondered what was wrong. . . .

On that note of confusion, Bella's passionate love affair with Edward Cullen began in TWILIGHT, Stephenie Meyer's bestselling first novel, published by Little, Brown and Company in October 2005. Bella would learn that Edward had been alive since 1901 and would be forever seventeen, the age at which he was changed into a vampire by Dr. Carlisle Cullen. Carlisle's coven included his partner, Esme, and the others Bella had gawked at that first day at Forks High: Alice and Emmett Cullen, and Rosalie and Jasper Hale. They adhered to Carlisle's principled philosophy of coexistence with humans and "vegetarian" vampirism (when they hunted, it was only for the blood of wild animals). But

Bella tested Edward's discipline—his hostile behavior was an anguished reaction to her intoxicating aroma, his instinctive lust for her blood. Edward struggled with the monster within, but Bella saw only his beautiful soul. Theirs would be the tension of two worlds aligning—he wanting her to preserve her mortality, she desiring to join him in eternal youth.

Readers knew the unlikely romance of Bella and Edward would one day have a reckoning. After TWILIGHT, two more novels followed. NEW MOON, published in September 2006, saw the sweethearts suffer a separation that drove Bella to despair and Edward to near-suicide. In ECLIPSE, published in September 2007, the vengeful vampire Victoria

How WOULD IT ALL *end?*

unleashed an army of bloodthirsty newborns to kill Bella. Bella survived to see Edward slide a ring on the fourth finger of her left hand.

Besides the long-awaited wedding, there was another big reason to anticipate the next installment—it was announced as the last. Would the marriage come off as planned, and would Edward keep his promise to "change" Bella? What of Bella's family and friends who knew nothing of this shadow world she had entered? What about Jacob Black, the Quileute tribe member who had inherited the ancient tribal power to "phase" into a wolf, and his unrequited love for Bella? And what of the Volturi, ancient rulers of the vampire world who had their own designs on Bella? How would it all *end?*

Edward helps Bella pack up her high school—and human—memories.

"BREAKING DAWN is a real departure from the first three books. It's a very adult story, a grown-up story. It's about leaving home and becoming a spouse and a parent—those are very adult issues. It becomes less about teen love and more about the complexities of a relationship in a marriage."

—MELISSA ROSENBERG, SCREENWRITER

Family and friends give the happy couple a big send-off.

production designer Richard Sherman, film editor Virginia Katz, and composer Carter Burwell. Other production principals were renowned for their work on epic, effects-laden fantasy films, including director of photography Guillermo Navarro, who shot *Hellboy* and its sequel, and *Pan's Labyrinth* (for which he won an Oscar®); costume designer Michael Wilkinson, who costumed the fighting Spartans and Persians of *300* and the superheroes of *Watchmen*; and veteran visual effects supervisor John Bruno, who had recently completed work on the epic *Avatar*.

"We wanted to go out with a bang," declared producer Wyck Godfrey, a veteran of all *The Twilight Saga* productions. "We wanted to step it up with the best artists we could get to bring closure to the franchise and the story of Bella, Edward, and Jacob. The first concern was finding a director we all believed in. We had chased Bill Condon before, and, lo and behold, this time he said yes. He had a clear

"WE WANTED TO GO OUT WITH A BANG."

vision for Bella's journey, and a deep understanding of the adult themes."

"As the franchise has developed, the spectacle quotient has escalated," observed Phil Tippett, whose Tippett Studio created the wolves throughout the series. "As the films draw to a close, there's a ramp-up in not only scale and spectacle but in subject matter—stuff gets pretty darn wild!"

Contrary to media speculation, splitting BREAKING DAWN into two movies was not a slam-dunk decision. Even producing one film was not an immediate green light. Screenwriter Melissa Rosenberg, after scripting all the previous *Twilight Saga* films, had decided to move on, while Stephenie Meyer herself had creative trepidations about the final chapter.

Before a BREAKING DAWN film could proceed, any creative concerns had to be resolved. If it was going to be done, it had to be done right.

The Equation

> "I was a still photographer when I had my first experience on a film set. I saw the difficulty of making a moving picture—solving that equation really puzzled me. There are so many elements involved, it's a miracle to sort out that equation and get a good shot. On that first set I got my complete intoxication with moving pictures."
>
> —GUILLERMO NAVARRO, DIRECTOR OF PHOTOGRAPHY

It had been an intense few years for Melissa Rosenberg, who was not only scripting *The Twilight Saga* but also working as head writer and executive producer on the Showtime cable series *Dexter* (about a blood analyst who moonlights as a vigilante killer). By the fall and winter of 2009, Rosenberg found herself at a crossroads—and looming on the creative horizon was the biggest blank page of all, a film adaptation of that epic fourth and final novel, BREAKING DAWN. "I had done three *Twilight* movies; I was pretty sure I wasn't going to do *Breaking Dawn*," she said.

Stephenie Meyer was going through her own creative conflict. The crux of her concerns, Rosenberg noted, was a key confrontation in BREAKING DAWN that the author wanted played without adding bloodshed. But Rosenberg felt that what amounted to "an intense conversation" that worked in a novel was not visually and dramatically compelling enough for the big screen. *The Twilight Saga: Breaking Dawn* was on hold until the story was resolved—and so Meyer and Rosenberg met for dinner at a Vancouver steakhouse. "That issue was going to decide whether either one of us was going to do this," Rosenberg recalled.

Over the course of dinner, their brainstorming session ended in a creative solution that made sense to both, breaking the impasse all around. "Summit was determined to make this movie, and I'm sure they would have managed to appease Stephenie without me or a steak dinner," Rosen-

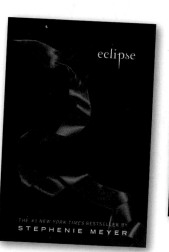

The four core novels of Stephenie Meyer's series, THE TWILIGHT SAGA, *published by Megan Tingley Books.*

berg said. "But she wouldn't have let anybody do the book if she didn't know it was going to be resolved, that the movie would stay true to her novel. I also realized I wanted to see it through and write 'The End' on it."

"Stephenie had to sign off on a choice, as did we all," producer Godfrey added. "One of the earliest conversations we had was whether she wanted BREAKING DAWN to become a movie, and how to do it properly, whether that meant one film or two. The truth is, I had concerns, [producer] Karen [Rosenfelt] had concerns, Melissa and everyone through the various stages of figuring it out had concerns about whether it was right to do one movie or two. The most important thing to all of us was that each movie had to be dramatically sound."

In her outline stage, Rosenberg quickly

> ## "THE MOST IMPORTANT THING TO ALL OF US WAS THAT EACH MOVIE HAD TO BE DRAMATICALLY SOUND."

realized that a single film would sacrifice too much story. "In BREAKING DAWN we had too much material for one movie, but just enough to make two! The main thing we would have lost by doing a single film was spending time with the wedding and honeymoon. No one wanted to blast through that—it was the culmination of several movies, and rich and beautiful and fun! A first film also allowed room for some invention, to push what was already suggested, such as the conflict between the wolves and the Cullens. One of the final deciding points for me was that the second half of the novel would have had to be condensed too much to get into one movie."

"One of my prerequisites when I signed on was I wasn't going to write two mediocre movies. If I could have made one great movie, Summit would have gone for it. I wasn't being forced to do two movies, and I did not feel pressured. Stephenie had approval and was willing to make a deal for this book, but [it was] predicated on whether it made sense to do one movie or two. So there was a lot riding on those first two outlines!"

—MELISSA ROSENBERG, SCREENWRITER

Stephenie Meyer on the set of Breaking Dawn, *playing the role of a wedding guest.*

"When Bill Condon came in, he said, 'I've come late to the game, but now I've *imprinted* on this material.' He identified *Breaking Dawn* as [being] about closure and propelling Edward and Bella into marriage, parenthood, and themes way more adult than in the first three films. He spoke with such eloquence about that transition and about the levels that it would take for Kristen to relate to being married. For him to watch Kristen through the first three films, and think about where she would need to go as an actress in *Breaking Dawn*, was an exciting proposition for him."

—WYCK GODFREY, PRODUCER

She wrote the outline for *Part 1* first, then *Part 2*. The screenplays themselves were a methodical process, with Rosenberg switching back and forth between drafts of the first film, then the second. The creative demands of writing two movies simultaneously compelled Rosenberg to, with regrets, leave *Dexter* in October 2009. Throughout that fall and winter, Rosenberg was "noodling around with possible approaches," and started to put her ideas on paper in November. That winter Summit began its search for a director, and when Bill Condon came aboard he began working with Rosenberg on her outlines. "I recall the outlines were approved, and Stephenie signed off on them, the beginning of March 2010," Rosenberg said.

Rosenberg found a natural ending for the first film around the novel's midpoint, after newlywed Bella, practically overnight, becomes pregnant, endures an accelerated and excruciating labor process, and seemingly dies giving birth. "Melissa was so fantastic in cracking the story, to feel you had closure at the end of *Part 1* when, in reality, both films are part of the same book," Godfrey said. "Once Melissa laid out how the novel could be split, it was a quick decision—let's do it! We decided to make both movies in one production period. It didn't make sense to come back a year later to shoot *Part 2*. The bigger the production gets, the harder it is to pull together all the people required to make the movie. It was more efficient to shoot both films simultaneously."

Feedback from Meyer (who has a producer credit on the film), producers Godfrey and Rosenfelt, and Condon led to the pivotal conflict of the first film. Initially, Rosenberg

Director Bill Condon on set with Taylor Lautner and Julia Jones.

wanted to have the Volturi, who figure prominently in *Part 2*, as a major presence in *Part 1*, an idea inspired by a Chapter 27 scene in which Bella receives a gem-studded box holding a jeweled necklace, a wedding gift from the feared Volturi leader, Aro. "My idea was that one of the Volturi would accompany the necklace [to Forks], and how would you keep Bella's pregnancy from them? It's not a big deal in the book; I was just looking for something to heighten the danger and threat while she's pregnant. But Bill and the producers started saying that bringing in the Volturi that early felt forced, that the real conflict in the book [for *Part 1*] was between the Cullens and the wolves. Although it doesn't go as far in the book, it's an interesting threat and involved Jacob leaving the pack to protect Bella." The result would be a climactic battle in the first movie, as the wolves attack the Cullen house, seeking to destroy Bella's baby.

By June 2010, Rosenberg had both scripts in good shape. She spent the summer working closely with the director, whom she refers to, in TV-speak, as a one-man "writer's room."

"In my opinion, Summit did a great job choosing the directors. I've had a great collaboration with each of them, but the collaboration with Bill has been the most enriching to me as a writer. He's an Academy Award®–winning screenwriter and knows whereof he speaks. At one point, I asked Bill if he wanted to do a pass, and he said no. He was very clear that I was going to write the screenplay, and he brought my game up. He focused on the right issues—

Staging victims of the Volturi on set.

Photo by John Bruno

characters, emotional arcs, the emotions of a scene. We had meetings lasting hours where he'd hone things, going over every line of the script.

"In particular, we went over and over the battle with the wolves, and the delicate scene where Edward asks Jacob to convince Bella not to have her baby. Bill put everything aside to concentrate on the story because a writer/director understands that without a script, you don't have a movie."

"BILL PUT EVERYTHING ASIDE TO CONCENTRATE ON THE STORY BECAUSE A WRITER/DIRECTOR UNDERSTANDS THAT WITHOUT A SCRIPT, YOU DON'T HAVE A MOVIE."

The variables facing each department—the sum total of factors needed to bring the latest TWILIGHT chapter to life—were immense and intense. For cinematographer Guillermo Navarro, the equation included camera setups, light manipulation, staging and composition, action, and getting it all as an image on film. For costume designer Michael Wilkinson, it was every stitch of clothing worn by anyone caught in the unblinking eye of Navarro's camera lens. For visual effects supervisor John Bruno, it was blending real and digital imagery into a seamless whole. In the end, the movie itself was the ultimate equation.

When the costume designer first met with the director, he discovered they were both fascinated by the global popularity of the novels—they could "ignite" the *Breaking Dawn* movies by tapping into that phenomenon.

Sarah Clarke as Bella's mom, Renée, and Kristen Stewart as Bella, discussing a scene with director Bill Condon.

"When you make a film as epic as this, it's important to be on the same page with the other departments. I not only worked closely with the director, but the DP [director of photography], the production designer, the props department, the hair and makeup. There were a lot of meetings and sharing of drawings and reference pictures. We made sure we discussed everything in detail before the first day of shooting. I try to not be overwhelmed by the immensity of the task, by the combined effect of the different departments going toward what you eventually see captured in the frame of the movie."

—MICHAEL WILKINSON, COSTUME DESIGNER

Bella wore an alternate wedding dress in a dream sequence.

"We wanted to break new ground in the series," Wilkinson explained. "Bill Condon and I felt it would be even more powerful if you could believe these characters could walk down the street, yet they have these amazing backgrounds of being a vampire or a shape-shifter. We gave the previous films a lot of respect and careful thought, while wanting to tell our story in the strongest and most engrossing way. Our approach was to look at why the audience connects so strongly. Our motivation was to make the characters and situations jump off the screen and do justice to the energy the books have created around the world."

The heart of the saga lies in the romantic and emotional dynamics of that storied threesome of Bella, Edward, and Jacob. One of the attractions of the project for Bill Condon was directing Kristen Stewart through Bella's emotional journey. "*Breaking Dawn* is a good companion piece to the first film because it's the completion of Bella's personal story, without the intrusion of outside forces or threats from the likes of the Volturi," Condon explained. "[*Breaking Dawn Part 2*] has an epic scale of vampires from across the globe and across many centuries coming together for one big battle, but in [*Part 1*] it's all Bella; it's about her getting married, becoming pregnant, and delivering a child."

> "WE GAVE THE PREVIOUS FILMS A LOT OF RESPECT AND CAREFUL THOUGHT, WHILE WANTING TO TELL OUR STORY IN THE STRONGEST AND MOST ENGROSSING WAY."

"I've been a fan of Kristen's since the first *Twilight* movie, and the other work she has done. Bella goes through so many changes, she has such an incredible arc across these two films, and to be part of helping Kristen take that journey was incredibly exciting. I think she is a great actress."

—BILL CONDON, DIRECTOR

Director Bill Condon on set with Kristen Stewart and Robert Pattinson, rehearsing some of their key scenes together.

Taylor Lautner as Jacob Black. "It was awesome for me as an actor to try to bring alive the old version of Jacob and now his new, mature side," said Lautner.

As many on the production observed, *The Twilight Saga: Breaking Dawn* was a thematic leap, with Bella and Edward facing new responsibilities as husband and wife. Jacob discovers he is a born leader, an Alpha male of the Quileute wolf pack. And despite the pain of rejection, Jacob joins Edward to be at Bella's side when her pregnancy threatens her life. During that ordeal, something like friendship—or perhaps just mutual respect— grows between the two bitter rivals.

"In the *Breaking Dawn* films, Edward, like Bella, goes through his own visual transformation," Wilkinson said. "He's going through the process of becoming an adult and facing more adult responsibility, becoming a husband and learning about that. By the end of the second film he will become a lot more self-aware and grown-up, which is a strange thing to say about someone who has already been on the planet for [more than] a century! Visually, we really wanted him to develop, to show a growing maturity throughout the films. The same way Edward matures, Jacob also starts making his own decisions. So we wanted to see Jacob in a more grown-up choice of clothes, less cutoffs and more flannel sleeved shirts."

Wilkinson began his work on *The Twilight Saga: Breaking Dawn* in June 2010 in Los Angeles, where he "shopped closets" for initial

Kristen Stewart as Bella, trying on her wedding shoes with Alice, played by Ashley Greene.

fittings for Stewart, Pattinson, Lautner, and the other Cullen family actors. The racks of clothes would "start a dialogue" and explore potential ensembles, right down to colors and textures. The Bella character alone had more than sixty costumes for both films, and Edward's wardrobe was not far behind, Wilkinson estimated.

"I think my main reason for loving doing what I do is I'm fascinated by people," Wilkinson reflected. "I think a costume designer is someone who is attracted to working out what makes people tick and exploring people's psychology. What costume designers do is give visual clues to characters through their choice of clothes, helping to tell the story and support the themes. I start with the script and absorb that. I do research and discuss the scenes with the director, providing support images appropriate to that discussion. I then start clothes fittings to explore a character with an actor. The tools we use will be the 'silhouettes,' which is the general shape of a costume, and colors and textures that help describe the character. I propose the final costumes. We then build from scratch, buy, or rent to alter."

Integral to the actors' looks were the hair and makeup departments. The task for hair alone was so large, with two movies shooting simultaneously, that stylist Rita Parillo became a coordinator to get the principal actors through and on camera in a timely manner. "The hair

Below: Jackson Rathbone as Jasper Hale with Greene as Alice Cullen.
Right: Kiowa Gordon as Embry Call.

department works with the director, costume, makeup, and the actors to come up with a look for each character," Parillo said. "When all was said and done, we had over forty wigs and hairpieces established, just for our principal cast. When second-unit stunt work started, we had to add another entire crew, with some workdays having as many as twenty hairstylists and seventy-five hairpieces. We had to establish a 'Wig Clean-Up Crew' headed by Monty Schuth to come in as sort of a second shift to clean, block, and set all the wigs and hairpieces and have them ready for the next day's work."

"When I was hired on, the director wanted the vampires to have a different look, more natural and organic," said Jean Black, makeup department head. "The vampires [in *The*

Twilight Saga] are unique in that they can walk among humans and adapt to the latest trends in the culture, so that's why we dialed things down to a more natural look. Making people pale was actually a more difficult task than I thought, especially with men. You are, in essence, creating a palette with little shape or contour. It can get theatrical very quickly, so every attempt was made to have a relatively new look while using less makeup and still keeping the integrity of what had gone before. We used a silicon-based makeup that was actually a spray-on, but which we discovered was easier to apply using a brush or sponge. It gave this smooth, stony-white feel the director wanted. The makeup also held up very well in the difficult elements we encountered, such as rain."

"WE DIALED THINGS DOWN TO A MORE NATURAL LOOK."

The look of the film also began in Los Angeles, with production designer Richard Sherman and art department head Lorin Flemming sketching such new concepts as the back of the Cullen house and Carlisle's study. "The production designer is responsible for the literal translation of the script, visually, either through sets we build or find on location," Sherman explained. "I work in conjunction with what the director is looking for, what I'm looking for, and what the story is looking for. I work with a lot of departments, but the two major ones are the art department, which acts like an architectural firm in getting sets built, and the set decoration department, who are like interior decorators on a set."

Digital technology has given all filmmakers a bigger toolbox, and the art department not only made physical models for sets, but also 3-D models that allowed for virtual walk-throughs. Their work defined the look of a set and what was needed to create it, in the process informing the needs of departments ranging from cinematography to location scouting. "I take Richard's artistic and stylish sense and funnel it down into a precise plan so it can be built," Flemming said. "I make sure I have all the parameters and information for construction to make it. Models help figure out the layout and space and how it's going to be constructed. I also try to make the models moody and evocative of what's going to be in there."

Principal set decorator David Schlesinger, an East Coast–based artist, admitted that

The Twilight Saga was a new world to him—the closest he had previously come was happening upon huge opening-day lines for *The Twilight Saga: Eclipse* at a movie theater in Union Square in Manhattan. "I was surprised a little bit. 'What is *this*? What's this all about?' Sure enough, I've become part of it all! But we all felt a real responsibility to the fans to not disappoint them, especially with the wedding. We took that very seriously.

"As a set decorator, I'm given an empty canvas," Schlesinger added. "I'm responsible for everything between the floor and the

> "BUT WE ALL FELT A REAL RESPONSIBILITY TO THE FANS TO NOT DISAPPOINT THEM, ESPECIALLY WITH THE WEDDING."

ceiling, from the furniture to the paper clips on a desk—everything that goes into a set to make it a real space. We put so much effort into finding the perfect whatever-it-is to dress a set. Decorating is about making decisions, and everything is a decision. This project was unique in that it's a fantasy. The Cullen house, especially, created a lot of challenges. One of the tricks we do on a regular set is to leave a drinking glass or coffee mug behind, or food in the kitchen—but these people don't eat; they have different habits. It was a constant reminder."

The Cullen house is the central location of the events in The Twilight Saga: Breaking Dawn Part 1. *The production researched medical equipment to dress the set of Carlisle Cullen's office.*

Director of photography Guillermo Navarro avoided sequels until he worked with director Guillermo Del Toro on the *Hellboy* films, which are based on the supernatural comic-book series by Mike Mignola. But this series was three films in, with three different directors and two different cinematographers. "It became a very interesting proposition to me," Navarro recalled. "How do I receive this plate that's been touched and cooked in different ways? I was debating with myself, but once I met with Bill Condon I knew a very strong collaboration was going to be possible. In *Breaking Dawn* there's a very dramatic change; everything in the series had been building up to this, and there was a huge opportunity to propel it forward. We went through tests with the production designer, the costume designer—all the visual aspects that have to work together were part of it. The aim was to carry a very strong visual presentation."

Navarro's interest in making images began when he was thirteen and started doing still photography, processing his pictures in a darkroom he had made in a closet of his Mexico home. Self-taught, he earned a livelihood doing everything from photojournalism to fashion photography before he moved on to making photographic images that *moved*. "The light and the frame and everything have to work for one moment, where you plan or capture everything that gravitates to the best image. There are too many choices, and more opportunities for error than to do it right. The equation to sorting it all out includes how light plays from different perspectives from the lens, the composition of the moving parts, the focus. So many elements are involved; it's a miracle when you get a good shot. But it's second nature to me now. I can see the shot, and what are the pieces to put it together."

The tools of a cinematographer's trade—lighting setups, tracks and cranes, cameras that range from handheld jobs to bulky Steadicams that look like something Iron Man might strap on—all have to work in service of the story. "I'm not there to do pretty images per se," Navarro declared. "A primary focus is not only creating the images but trying to find the visual language the movie needs. The visual language for a film has its own grammar and its own rules. It's where and why the camera moves, it's keeping

"I consider myself a storyteller with images. There's a big difference between just capturing an image as it goes by and creating a reality through the lens. Movies allow you to create a parallel reality that doesn't belong to the everyday life you live. Creating reality from scratch is appealing to me. For that you have to be in complete control of your domain and the exercise of the film language."

—GUILLERMO NAVARRO, DIRECTOR OF PHOTOGRAPHY

the relationship of the actors correct in terms of storytelling, it's creating an atmosphere and the look of the story."

"As far as the 'look' of movie one, I wanted to do a genre that's really discredited, and that is the romantic melodrama," Condon explained. "For example, there's a very specific use of color to track Bella's emotional states, while the camera work is, I would say, immersive. Also, unlike the other books, which are told from Bella's point of view, there's a chunk of BREAKING DAWN told from Jacob's point of view, so we wanted to get inside what it's like to be a wolf with a pack. We wanted to get inside both of those characters, to see their stories from the inside out. For example, when Bella realizes she's pregnant, the camera starts behind her as she slowly looks down to her stomach and touches it; the camera comes around and she's looking into the mirror, for the first time, as a mother. You're inside her head."

All the disparate elements of *The Twilight Saga: Breaking Dawn* would come together in the digital editing suite of editor Virginia Katz, one of Condon's regular collaborators. Although

Bella realizes something is different.

*From left: Gaffer
David Lee, director
of photography
Guillermo Navarro,
Pattinson, and Stewart
go over the birth.*

29

Robert Pattinson as Edward.

her father, Sidney Katz, was a film editor (his credits include the 1970 drama *Diary of a Mad Housewife*), she didn't necessarily want to take up the family business. "I never thought I'd want to be an editor; I didn't even know the kind of work it was. One summer my parents decided to not let me hang out with friends on the beach. Dad had his own company and was quite busy supervising several movies, so I came to help. Two weeks in, my father began handing me scenes to cut. I went in thinking it would be a summer job. I never left."

Katz would see her field transition from the photochemical medium of celluloid to the computer age, where film is transferred into digital form onto such "non-linear" editing machines as the Avid. The last movie she cut with film was director Condon's 1995 release *Candyman: Farewell to the Flesh*. "I loved film, but as more and more companies were moving to Avid systems, I did also. On *Candyman*, there was so much film that I realized the benefits of digital editing. I wouldn't have to wait for a trim to be handed to me. I didn't have to worry about shredding the film—or my fingers, for that matter. I learned the Avid and I've never looked back!

"A film editor's job is to tell the story in the clearest way possible," Katz explained. "Film has a rhythm and a pace. It's my job to find the timing within each scene. *Breaking Dawn* was unusual in that we shot two movies at the same time. That meant I was editing two movies at the same time. But working with Bill Condon is an editor's dream. He is supportive and generous, always open to ideas. We've worked together for many years, and we trust each other, which is key to getting a result we're both happy with. While he was shooting I would put the film together and feed him cut scenes throughout the shoot, so he would know what he was getting. By the time we sat down in the cutting room together [in postproduction], he knew the cut film as well as I did. My assistants did a great job keeping the continuity in order and feeding me film constantly. Not only was there practical footage, but a lot of visual effects to consider."

After the director, one of the first hires was visual effects supervisor John Bruno, who had spent a year working on greenscreen soundstages in New Zealand for *Avatar*. After that monumental assignment, Bruno was looking forward to having some "chill" time but agreed to discuss *The Twilight Saga: Breaking Dawn* over breakfast with Godfrey and Condon. An admitted "envelope pusher," he felt that *The Twilight Saga* world was set on the visual effects side, from occasional vampire sparkle to the CG (computer generated) wolves. Nevertheless, he read the script for *Part 1*, and in the third-act sequence of Bella's pregnancy, he saw a chance to do some envelope pushing. As effects supervisor on *X-Men: The Last Stand* (2006), Bruno had worked with Lola Visual Effects, whose proprietary "digital skin grafting" system thinned twenty years off the faces of actors Ian McKellen and Patrick Stewart, and he wanted to do something similar for Bella's pregnancy, along with "old-school" makeup and practical effects.[6]

"In terms of Bella, you meet Prince Charming, you have this romantic royal wedding, you go on this spectacular honeymoon on an island, you get pregnant . . . and you *die*!" Bruno marveled. "I signed on. I was hired before the DP or the production designer. The first thing I did was get feedback on the script for Bill and started storyboarding and doing pre-viz [previsualization]. Visual effects is very involved with other departments. I love collaborating with the art department, and I consider Richard Sherman one of the best. I also work very closely with the director of photography, and we had a great one in Guillermo Navarro." Confident that Tippett Studio had the wolves under control, Bruno would bring aboard John Rosengrant of Legacy Effects to create the special makeup appliances and prosthetics for Bella's physical deterioration, with Lola Visual Effects taking her emaciated look to the limit. Using previsualization—a low-resolution computer graphics version of a potential scene—they planned Bella's physical decline.

Bruno was also the perfect resource for a director who was generally unfamiliar with the often counterintuitive world of visual effects. "I'm bringing Bill into this world kicking and screaming!" Bruno said with a laugh. "He's truly focused on character, and a terrific writer and storyteller. But the shots of Kristen thinning raised the bar, story-wise. We had so many visual effects shots. *Eclipse* had something like two hundred and fifty; on *Breaking Dawn* we've got from seven hundred and fifty to nine hundred on the first movie alone."

As befit the biggest novel in the series, *The Twilight Saga: Breaking Dawn* was the franchise's biggest production. As stunt coordinator Scott Ateah put it, "A big movie is like a snowball running downhill—it keeps getting bigger and bigger."

Visual effect supervisor John Bruno.

The Blueprint

The Cullen house exterior.

33

"I stayed out of that loop for quite some time while the issue of doing one movie or two ping-ponged back and forth. After the dust settled I could move forward with designing a blueprint according to the master plan approved by all. The blueprint took into account the dynamics of two movies, and variables that had to be defined, such as whether to shoot separately or 'block shoot' in one location. I got clarity from the core team and designed a blueprint that worked."

—BILL BANNERMAN, CO-PRODUCER AND AERIAL UNIT DIRECTOR

Shooting two films simultaneously required an international production, with a nearly two-thousand-person crew for all units, estimated Bill Bannerman, who was responsible for "bringing all the tools together," as he put it, a role he had been performing since *New Moon*. Bannerman termed the daunting logistics of putting all the pieces in place "the blueprint."

While awaiting resolution of the early debate about making BREAKING DAWN into one film or two, the production had a few markers for the journey ahead: They knew time was tight; they were likely to shoot in another country; and their base of operations would shift from Vancouver, the primary production base since *New Moon*, to Louisiana. "The decision to go to Louisiana was purely based on the financial benefits—Louisiana has an incredible tax-rebate system," producer Godfrey explained. "A lot of movies have shot there in the last four to five years. There was a really strong crew

Billy Burke with Stewart, as father and daughter.

"This project reminded me of what it must have been like to make *Gone with the Wind*. You're always dealing with the drama in front of you, but there's also the fact that you want to fulfill the expectations of the people who have read the books. Kristen took that especially seriously. She almost tortured herself, wanting to be the vessel to express the many emotions of her character. Kristen is so self-reliant, but my role was to help her and the other actors as their first audience, the first set of eyes, encouraging all the things they could bring to their characters. "

—BILL CONDON, DIRECTOR

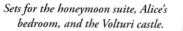

*Sets for the honeymoon suite, Alice's
bedroom, and the Volturi castle.*

[to draw from] in Louisiana, and we
could also pull from Atlanta—it's like
Hollywood South."

Bill Bannerman's blueprint included
prep time for deciding the creative
issues before principal photography
began in November 2010. "Normally,
you have twenty weeks of prep, but
we had approximately fourteen
to fifteen weeks, and a lot of questions to
be answered," Bannerman noted. "We had to
work out the dynamics needed to deliver all the
dramatic beats."

The blueprint for shooting two films simultaneously included "block shooting," where
scenes from both movies occurring at the same
location were scheduled together for maximum
efficiency. "I remember when, within the space
of a couple days, Kristen went from the married
Bella to pregnant Bella to vampire Bella, with
major makeup changes going on all the time,"
Bill Condon recalled. "What was helpful was
that early on I'd put both scripts together on

my iPad, so it was like we were
making one big, two-hundred-page
screenplay. That focused the idea that both
movies were connected."

With the release dates in mind, a hundred-
day schedule was drawn up—fifty days for each
film. The blueprint for interior soundstage sets
was driven by what would take the longest to
build and demand the most filming time, and
that was the Cullen house. "Almost three-quarters
of the scenes in both movies take place in the
Cullen house or its surroundings," art director

THE BLUEPRINT

35

"The Cullen house is the icon for this franchise. Unbeknownst to the fans, we had the Cullen house set from *Eclipse* traveling cross-country from Vancouver. Fans might even have passed all these semi-trailers in which the Cullen house was enclosed, on its way to be rebuilt in Baton Rouge."

—BILL BANNERMAN, CO-PRODUCER AND AERIAL UNIT DIRECTOR

Flemming noted. What Bannerman called the "interior blueprint . . . the multitude of equations" for shooting the interior sets revolved around the Cullen house that had been built for *The Twilight Saga: Eclipse*. That stage set was designed to be taken apart, stored, and put back together for the next movie.

Prior to starting on the Cullen house, smaller sets were done, including interiors for Bella's house, the honeymoon house, Alice's bedroom (where Bella gets ready for her wedding), and the Volturi chamber. Those and other sets were built in an industrial warehouse in Port Allen, a town across the Mississippi River from Baton Rouge. The owner had been loathe to rent it—a previous film production had "burned locations," Bannerman recalled, meaning they had trashed the place. After convincing the owner that *The Twilight Saga* team was professional and respectful of its stage space, the crew began converting for film work. "We turned that industrial warehouse into a poor man's soundstage," Bannerman said. "When you go into an empty warehouse [not built for filmmaking], it becomes a construction zone because you have to build an overhead lighting grid system and bring in equipment. After two weeks the owner came by and was in wonder at how clean we'd kept it; he felt we were totally professional. When we left, you wouldn't have known we were there."

The problem with the *The Twilight Saga: Eclipse* Cullen house, Bannerman observed, was that the gigantic set, comprising two of the house's imagined three stories, exceeded height limits on about ninety percent of the soundstage and warehouse space in Louisiana. There was a big enough stage at the new Celtic Media Centre in Baton Rouge, but that was already occupied by *Battleship*, another big production. The soundstage they were searching for also needed to be near deciduous trees, stand-ins for a forest indigenous to the Pacific Northwest for a major scene in the second movie.

Bannerman's focus was the state's three big cities: New Orleans, Baton Rouge, and Shreveport. The scouting mission sometimes found a forest, but no nearby stage space. New Orleans had a forest north of Lake Pontchartrain, but the production couldn't risk potential closings of causeways out of the Big Easy.

Then the production got lucky. In a case of fortuitous timing, Celtic Media Centre was nearing completion on another major stage at its Baton Rouge facility, and it was a perfect fit for the Cullen house. The stage was finished and available by September 2010, and two weeks later the production was setting up the set,

> "THE CULLEN HOUSE IS CRAZY. I THINK WE'VE BUILT THAT SET AS MANY DIFFERENT WAYS AS YOU COULD POSSIBLY BUILD IT."

which had been transported from Vancouver. It took six forty-foot trucks to hold it all, Bannerman recalled, from walls and flooring to cedar siding, windows, doors, and railings.

The house described in the novel is deep in primordial woods, a three-story place that is a century old. But the first movie presented a modern structure of glass surfaces and polished concrete floors, an actual home in Portland owned by a Nike executive. Audiences for the first film did not see much of the exterior—the house was built into a hillside, not surrounded by forest. But the look of the house set the style for the films to come.

The Cullen house was prominently featured in *The Twilight Saga: Eclipse*, notably as the setting for the Forks High graduation party. Producer Wyck Godfrey had imagined an outdoor set, but *Eclipse* production designer Paul Austerberry proposed re-creating the Portland house indoors. After gathering the necessary data, photographs, and permission from the house's architects, two

Bella rests in the Cullen living room on the two-story interior set.

Edward watches from inside the Cullen home . . .

"Stephenie's great. I can't thank her enough. She created these characters, and having her on set for these movies has been amazing because whenever you need anything, have any questions...Let's face it, this is probably the most confusing, complicated movie yet. It's been awesome to be able to go up to her at any given moment and ask her anything....She's actually a little prankster. She's quite funny. So I've had a lot of fun with her, and I think everybody's grown pretty close to her."

—TAYLOR LAUTNER, ACTOR

...Jacob guards the outside.

stories were built on a twenty-thousand-square-foot Vancouver soundstage, complete with interior space, a driveway, and surrounding forest and vegetation provided by the greens department.[7] In *Eclipse*, the Cullen house was used exclusively for night scenes, but it needed to be more versatile for *Breaking Dawn*, which required day scenes for the wedding and reception, to be held in the backyard of the Cullen home. "At night you have a little more flexibility to 'cheat' certain sets, but the sun can show the truth of a set," Bannerman observed.

The Cullen house for *Breaking Dawn* would be realized *twice*, once as the *Eclipse* interior set on the Baton Rouge soundstage, the other as a new two-story house built in the forest an hour and a half outside Vancouver. "The Cullen house is crazy. I think we've built that set as many different ways as you could possibly build it," Godfrey said. "It's been fun because every director has been able to bring in a new element to the house, just by continuing to add to it. In *Breaking Dawn* we see Alice's bedroom and the entire back exterior of the house. In short, the Cullen house is constantly under renovation."

The location set, roughly a half hour's drive out of Squamish, included a river, fully realizing Meyer's vision from the novels (a glimpse of the river in *Eclipse*, an effect on the soundstage set, had some fans clamoring to see more). Godfrey recalls being with the location scouting team outside Squamish, trying to imagine a massive house in the setting, along with a glittering wedding. The group included Condon, Bannerman, Sherman, location manager Abraham Fraser, supervising art director Jeremy Stanbridge, and construction coordinator Doug Hardwick. They decided, on the spot, not to divide filming between the daytime wedding at the location and the evening reception on a Vancouver soundstage. "We were standing in the woods and we knew we were going to leave and not be back for six months, so we had to make a call," Godfrey added. "We all said, 'Yeah, let's do it.' We decided not to split things up piecemeal but do the entire wedding reception outside."

"For this movie we needed to stage the wedding in the backyard of the Cullen house, with the river in the background. We really needed to do the whole thing because we'd be filming there for months. Ultimately, we needed a place that existed in reality, in a location that matched what had been established for the outside of the house, with this bucolic setting next to the river in the back. That's why we built the house in Canada for the exteriors, and took a very heavy greenscreen approach to interiors for the soundstage set."

—BILL CONDON, DIRECTOR

Rosalie (Nikki Reed, center) becomes one of Bella's strongest allies during the pregnancy.

The full location house would allow the first helicopter views of the house, river, and forest. Firsts for the house included a view of the back, Carlisle's ground-floor study, and Alice's third-floor bedroom. The third floor itself would also be seen—as a computer graphics set extension generated by John Bruno's department.

Movie magic would marry two separate sets that were thousands of miles apart. The *Eclipse* set in Baton Rouge was surrounded with greenscreen that would be digitally composited with plates shot at the forest location outside Squamish. (A term from the early days when still photography used negatives of sheets of glass, *plates* refers to the backgrounds filmed for a composite shot.) "There are so many scenes in the Cullen house, from the living room to the kitchen, all looking out the windows, that we needed it to look as real as possible," art director Flemming explained. "Visual effects are so good now, we decided to use greenscreen, so all the forest you see outside [the soundstage set] is from the actual forest on location."

"There was such an issue about reflections and lighting scenarios that we took the glass *out* of the soundstage set," John Bruno said. "The [simultaneous shooting] also got crazy. No one really knew what was outside the Cullen house set in terms of lighting. Is it raining, do we have wet trees? How much light from the house is illuminating the trees? It was determined that in order to keep blazing away, I would match whatever was out there with the real location and composite accordingly. I've always hated

expansive decks." The dual Cullen house sets were modified to serve Condon's story needs and the cinematographic needs of Guillermo Navarro. Modifications requested by the director included taking advantage of the house's depth and opening up the narrow hallway on the second floor to provide a more obvious connection between the kitchen and living room.

The big challenge for Sherman's art department—and Flemming's major task—was designing the back of the house. The art department looked at photo references and homes with architectural styles similar to that of the seminal Portland house. As a template, the art director took a 3-D computer model from previous films and began building a model based on the Portland location. "I work in SketchUp, an architectural design program made to be user-friendly and intuitive," Flemming said. "It has a sketchy feel to it, the natural process of an artist drawing on paper, but in 3-D. The trouble with digital art, I think, is the lines look so crisp and final in all stages of the process. This program captures the preliminary process of creation and allows you to make images that look more finite as the process itself gets more and more finite [as it arrives at the final image]."

Carlisle's study was built into both sets as part of the newly designed back of the house.

that whole 'fix it in post' thing. [But] in this case, that was a good solution. The set was in the middle of the stage in Baton Rouge, so we could surround it with three hundred and sixty degrees of greenscreen, about forty feet away. Throughout the shooting on location, there were rain and clouds; it was rare to see sun. I'd just grab a camera and shoot background plates to potentially go into these [lighting] scenarios for the house. Then, Mark Weingartner [visual effects director of photography] spent a week shooting plates, and finally got some sun plates."

Lorin Flemming estimated both sets at, roughly, 9,250 square feet, "including the

"WE WANTED TO KEEP CARLISLE'S STUDY AS OPEN AS POSSIBLE."

Because the abundance of glass allowed one to see both inside and outside, both sets had complete interiors, along with exteriors. "Because both houses had one story on top of the other, we had to build it like a real house, with structural integrity so one floor could support the other," Flemming added. "We knew we needed space to fit in Carlisle's office, so we pulled out a back section of the house for it. Then we built some large decks off the back of the house that cantilevered over the office, but kept to the diagonal lines inherent in that house, along with lots of glass. If you are facing the back of the house, with your back to the river, Carlisle's study is on the left side, below the huge upstairs back deck off the lounge and living room."

"We wanted to keep Carlisle's study as open as possible," Richard Sherman added. "We achieved an effect of openness in the background with glass looking out onto the forest. The study area has a sofa and a fireplace, a big desk, lots of floor-to-ceiling bookcases, and a kind of conference area. Bella actually has her baby in the fireplace area."

Turning the art department's detailed specs into reality were construction coordinators Randall Coe in Louisiana and Doug Hardwick in Canada. Hardwick's construction work at the Squamish set was accomplished in two phases,

"It was definitely challenging to one's creative stamina [working on two films simultaneously]. But it was important to all of us to get it right. That's what kept us going. The shooting was all mixed up. One day it was the wedding, the next Bella was giving birth to a half-vampire/half-human child, the next Esme was bringing sandwiches out to the werewolves in the garden of the Cullen house. You had to be on top of it, to know both scripts back to front."

—MICHAEL WILKINSON, COSTUME DESIGNER

Esme (Elizabeth Reaser) brings food out to the wolves guarding her house: Leah, Seth, and Jacob.

beginning in late September 2010. "We first cleared the site and began building the main structure, then sealed it up when the weather got bad in mid-December," Flemming recalled. "We came back in mid-January to complete the interior and add the finishing touches. It was challenging, because it was a very cold and snowy winter. I heard it was still under several feet of snow before they were supposed to shoot, and steam machines had to be brought in to melt the snow."

It was actually *five* feet of snow, Richard Sherman recalled. "A week before shooting at the Cullen house, an incredible storm came through. This was on a Monday, and we were supposed to film there the following Tuesday. But Doug Hardwick and Jeremy Stanbridge, our art director in Vancouver, made it happen. They brought in steam [to melt the snow] and created these verdant fields of ferns and green. Within the week, they made it look like summer. You'd never have known the place had been under five feet of snow. It was amazing."

While Sherman and Flemming spent a few weeks doing initial conceptual work in Los Angeles in June 2010, supervising art director Troy Sizemore went ahead to Baton Rouge to set up the art department. Flemming was ultimately stationed there, while Jeremy Stanbridge handled art department duties in Canada. In addition to a virtual 3-D model of the Cullen house, the art department crafted two scale foam-core models (the larger one at four feet by two feet, the smaller one at two and a half feet by one foot). As the other departments began arriving in Baton Rouge, the physical models provided a useful, hands-on reference.

That busy summer in Baton Rouge, the director and screenwriter worked on the final screenplay. John Bruno, already off and running, had assembled a departmental team he'd been working with for years, including visual effects producer Robin Griffin; visual effects coordinators Ron Moore and Suzanne Murarik; second-unit visual effects supervisor Terry Windell; and Mark Weingartner, who shot the VistaVision plates. The costume designer had moved from his "hunting and gathering" phase in Los Angeles to Louisiana, where camera tests homed in on the final costume looks. Navarro and his crew of fourteen years were developing the visual look. Set decorator David Schlesinger also set up shop in Baton Rouge, while another set director, Jan Blackie-Goodine, came on in January to lead set-dressing duties for the wedding and reception in Canada.

Blackie-Goodine, an art direction Oscar® nominee with production designer Henry Bumstead for Clint Eastwood's *Unforgiven*, had ideal experience for dressing a set in a forest at the tail end of the rainy season. "A lot of decorators are used to working within a city environment, and we were in a rain forest, an hour and a half out of Vancouver, in primitive, rough conditions," she said. "They needed someone who could work in those conditions—that would be me! I'm used to working in hot weather and when it's thirty degrees below. Being 'off the pavement' doesn't scare me. I come from a ranching family, but I'm a city girl, too—the best of both worlds. The production was also looking for someone with a feminine sensibility because the wedding had to be fairy tale–like and magical."

As the production finished prepping in Baton Rouge, filming began with four to five days in Brazil. The first unit then returned to Louisiana to shoot all interior work for both films and the lion's share of the schedule, which ran from November to mid-February. With a week to transition cast, crew, and equipment, principal photography spent thirty-eight days in British Columbia. At the end, the shooting schedule of one hundred days would be plus one, with an extra day added for a key honeymoon scene that finally wrapped principal photography for the entire franchise.

Co-producer Bannerman recalled the wedding as "quite the ordeal." Although Meyer's storybook wedding was set in August (August 13, to be exact), the production would be filming in a snow and rain belt. "We left the wedding to the end of principal photography because the rains don't stop until late May and we were wrapping in late April," Bannerman said. "The majority of our exteriors needed non-rain conditions, and we were in a place where it rains every day."

Of course, it wouldn't be a *Twilight Saga* production without tales to tell of stormy weather. Rough weather was unavoidable, given

Cloths were hung up to diffuse the light on exterior British Columbia locations.

"THE WEDDING HAD TO BE FAIRY TALE—LIKE AND MAGICAL."

the requisite locations needed to emulate rainy and overcast Forks and its environs. But it wasn't just local weather. Production designer Sherman noted, "We were shooting a scene [for *Part 1*] on Vancouver Island, and we were evacuated because of the tsunami that hit Japan!"

The wedding, coming at the end of the schedule, stayed uppermost in the minds of the production team throughout principal photography. Bella and Edward's nuptials was the big event that *The Twilight Saga: Breaking Dawn* production team—and the entire franchise—had been moving toward.

"The wedding was something we started thinking about from day one," David Schlesinger added. "We knew the importance of it—it terrified us, really. It was a huge responsibility because the fans had been waiting for this wedding for years and we knew we had to get it right. From the moment I started the job we were thinking about it."

A Midsummer Night's Dream

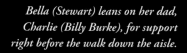
Bella (Stewart) leans on her dad, Charlie (Billy Burke), for support right before the walk down the aisle.

"There have been a billion weddings, basically rhapsodies on the same theme, with wide aisles, white chairs, and flowers. The idea for this wedding was it was this organic thing coming out of the forest. That led into this Midsummer Night's Dream idea. That ensued into everything being covered with moss, bent branches turned into seats covered with flowers and moss, the aisle covered with white flowers on moss, a [canopy] of wisteria as if it were raining flowers, all these white, wispy flowers mixed in with the pale and dark green of the forest."

—RICHARD SHERMAN, PRODUCTION DESIGNER

The stormy Olympic rain-forest region is integral to the world of *The Twilight Saga*, providing safe haven for the Cullens and Quileute wolves, but also cover for nomad vampires on the prowl—tranquility and threat coexist in the emerald depths. "The forest, with its huge, old-growth trees and ferns, almost becomes a character," said set decorator Jan Blackie-Goodine. "The forest has always played a huge part in the story, from the first film, and makes a beautiful and mysterious location for the Cullen house. The forest is also kind of terrifying. Because it rains so much, everything is covered in moss, which is parasitic. The moss crawls up the trees and ends up killing them—it's beautiful, in a very cruel way."

The quintessential forest has been an iconic setting in history and sacred writings, myths and fairy tales—a place of menace, mystery, and swashbuckling adventure. In Shakespeare's *A Midsummer Night's Dream*, the forest was a refuge for fairies and for the lovers Hermia and Lysander, a magical theme the production designer tapped into for Bella and Edward's wedding.

Richard Sherman had struggled to come up with an approach that would do justice to the event and salutes Aristotle Circa, a friend and fashion stylist, for offering the idea that unlocked the creative approach. "They're getting married out in the forest, so Ari said, 'Why don't you just have it growing out of the forest, like a natural thing?' Ari's suggestion was a big burden off my shoulders. That was the starting point. The Midsummer Night's Dream evolved out of that."

Bella's mom (played by Sarah Clarke) gets her wedding invitation in the mail.

ISABELLA MARIE SWAN

AND

EDWARD ANTHONY MASEN CULLEN

TOGETHER WITH THEIR FAMILIES

REQUEST THE HONOR OF YOUR PRESENCE

AT THE CELEBRATION OF THEIR MARRIAGE

SATURDAY, THE THIRTEENTH OF AUGUST

TWO THOUSAND AND ELEVEN

FIVE O'CLOCK IN THE EVENING

420 WOODCROFT AVE

FORKS, WA

Visions Did Appear

The film would have a Midsummer's Nightmare, as well. On the eve of their wedding, Edward gives Bella one last chance to understand the potential ramifications of becoming a vampire, and her subconscious fears play out in a dream sequence the production called the "nightmare wedding." At its height of horror, Bella finds herself standing atop the bloodied bodies of her friends and family, the corpses stacked like a wedding cake. The idea began with Condon's early conversations with Robert Pattinson, who was in touch with Edward's guilt and self-loathing from when he rebelled against Carlisle's doctrine of "vegetarian" vampirism.

"There was a period when Edward explored what it was like to kill humans and drink their blood," Condon said. "Although he was careful to only kill people who were killing other people, sort of the 'Dexter' of the 1930s, he realized he was a monster, he was still killing humans. So he came back to Carlisle and fully committed to the program. That felt like an interesting idea to explore on the last night before they get married. This is one last opportunity for him to lay out for Bella why she should really consider it, that she may not be able to control herself [as a vampire], that she may do terrible things she'll feel terrible about for the next hundred years. She dreams and imagines, in her Bella-like way, how she might be capable of that. . . . It's an example of getting to the essence of something visually."

At right, the on-site special effects foreman Heath Hood spreads the blood around the pileup of victims. Among them are Forks friends Mike Newton (Michael Welch), Jessica Stanley (Anna Kendrick), and Eric Yorkie (Justin Chon). Below right, actress Sarah Clarke takes her place on the pile. Below, Bella and Edward complete the nightmarish wedding cake.

Photo by John Bruno

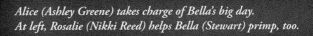

Alice (Ashley Greene) takes charge of Bella's big day.
At left, Rosalie (Nikki Reed) helps Bella (Stewart) primp, too.

As in the novel, Alice Cullen (Ashley Greene) happily jumps in as wedding planner, right down to designing Bella's wedding dress. "We wanted a wedding very specific to our world, one that Alice would design for her new sister-in-law with the utmost elegance and care," said Wilkinson. "In the book, Bella is out of her league thinking about planning a wedding; that's not really the way she rolls. Alice, of course, is only too keen to take over the role, and puts a lot of care into it. The Cullens have a love of the beauty of nature. There's the harmonious garden in the middle of the woods—it just wanted to have a very fresh, romantic, and young feel."

Bringing the Midsummer Night's Dream idea to life included creating prototypes of rough-hewn pews for the ceremony, made of branches and logs. These pews were designed at the Baton Rouge art department and built in Canada. The Vancouver-based set-decorating team created a canopy of wisteria for the ceremony. "Richard wanted it to look like it was raining flowers," Blackie-Goodine said.

The wisteria vines, designed to look real, were made of quality silk shipped in from silk floral shops all over the United States and Canada—almost five hundred vines, each eighteen feet long, with a six-person crew stripping off the leaves and leaving the blossoms. The riggers provided the canopy, and Blackie-Goodine's crew attached their wisteria-blossom vines to that. Sean Blackie, Jan's son and assistant, and Thomas Walker, lead set dresser, helped rig the canopy to cover the whole assembly, an area sixty by eighty feet square. "The rigging had to be very strong from the trees," Blackie-Goodine explained. "It was dangerous for the riggers who had to climb the trees—whenever there was a wind, the rigging they were stringing moved. It was stressful preparing the scene, but it all looked beautiful and ethereal. It was like part of the forest, a look we carried through to the reception."

An estimated fifteen to twenty prototype tables for the evening reception were considered, along with flowers and centerpieces. "We finally settled on something Richard [Sherman] and I were satisfied with," Schlesinger said. "We created a finer prototype of actual tables with flowers and all the elements and showed it to Bill Condon for his final approval. For the centerpieces we kept looking at flower arrangements in vases, and it always felt very formal. We started playing around a bit, taking flowers out of their vases and holding them up. We ended up making a mound of floral foam covered in moss, and put flowers into that. The idea was the flowers were growing up from the forest floor and out of the table."

The canopy for the evening wedding reception included cluster lights, a Christmas-lights effect that emulated the floating wisteria of the daytime wedding. "The greens department

"We wanted the wedding to seem like it was growing out of the ground where [the Cullens] live in this magical, enchanted forest. We wanted to have a bit of a magical feel to it. It's really about the best part of being a vampire, which is you live this enchanted, other existence."

—BILL CONDON, DIRECTOR

Emmett Cullen (Kellan Lutz) and Rosalie (Nikki Reed) carry "logs" to help set up for the wedding.

brought in truckloads of mosses and huge ferns and trees where there was bare space, so when we went to decorate, it was already so magical," Blackie-Goodine added. "It helped us, as set decorators, to add to the environment. Apart from the organic benches and hanging wisteria vines, white flowers were added in along with the ferns and the moss. It all became a study of green and white, very Midsummer Night's Dream."

The burden of staging the wedding and reception was an equation to be solved by all, beginning with screenwriter Rosenberg. "I wanted the wedding to be a huge event. There was a lot in the book, and I tried to include as much of that as possible, but to get it across without dialogue. The main part is the marriage ceremony, where dialogue is less

important than Edward and Bella and that moment at the altar. Jacob is also part of it, and there's the very important introduction of the Denali sisters, who have a long history with the Cullens and a rich backstory that plays out throughout the book. To get all of that in the wedding was very tricky."

"The wedding had different mandates to accomplish; we had a lot to do in a day and a half," Guillermo Navarro observed of the tight shooting schedule. "One mandate was it should not be [too] sunny because vampires sparkle in the sunlight. For the wedding, vampires and humans have to coexist, so I flew huge fabrics of diffusion that were incorporated into the set. There were big moments, like where Bella's father meets her [before the wedding

"My first meeting with Richard Sherman, he had really worked through the back-to-nature, Midsummer Night's Dream idea for the wedding. Ten months later the [production design] was still true to that central idea. The organic nature of everything was stunning, a real achievement. It felt like the world of *Twilight*."

—WYCK GODFREY, PRODUCER

Guillermo Navarro and Bill Condon on the wedding set in British Columbia. Below, Esme, Jasper, and Carlisle (Peter Facinelli) help build the outdoor wonderland.

ceremony].... There were shots where you had to see all the surroundings and design of that space. There was the dynamic of Bella walking in and meeting Edward, who is waiting for her. We did a shot where they're alone together, isolated from the witnesses and the party itself."

One unavoidable aspect of the wedding and reception shoot was heightened security. "Nothing prepared me for the security on this show," Blackie-Goodine said. "When we were filming, we were in lockdown. We always had security passes, but we also had to hand in all phones and cameras; we had to sign confidentiality agreements."

Bannerman, who was in charge of security, explained that the "extreme security protocol" was vital to protecting the integrity of the final film. *Everything* was a security element—Bella's wedding dress, Edward's tuxedo, the guests' outfits, the vows, the place settings, the wedding cake. Although the day of the wedding shoot was not announced, and was staged in a remote area, Bannerman estimated news of the event "went viral" within twenty-four to thirty-six hours. Twi-fans had spied actors playing Bella's former Forks High classmates departing LAX or arriving in Vancouver—in the novel, these characters appear only at the wedding—so the dots were connected. Text messaging spread the news of the shoot like virtual wildfire.

"They knew the actors were arriving for the wedding; that was one element of the cat being out of the bag," Bannerman noted. "This was

ONE UNAVOIDABLE
ASPECT OF THE
WEDDING AND
RECEPTION SHOOT WAS
HEIGHTENED SECURITY.

like a real celebrity wedding, where everyone wants a piece of the action. We had to control about twenty acres at all times so no images of the wedding would be a spoiler put out into the viral world. We had to keep prying eyes *out*, cameras *out*, electronics *out*. There was security there to preserve the moviegoing experience, the magic and wonderful way it was created. It had taken three movies to get to this point, and Bill Condon put a lot of thought into the sequence. It would have been a shame to see that compromised, to have that thunder stolen away by a picture or piece of information. Bill was very sensitive to that reality."

As befit the fairy-tale atmosphere, it had been raining up to the wedding day, when the rain suddenly stopped, the clouds parted, and the sun came out. It was sunny for two days, the time it took to shoot the ceremony. But when the big moment arrived, that which the production most feared happened: "We heard there were offers of a million dollars for a picture of the wedding dress," John Bruno recalled. "On the day we shot the wedding, Kristen walks out in the dress—which is *spectacular*—and a helicopter buzzes us and there's a guy hanging out of it! We could hear it coming, and someone shouted, 'Cover the dress!' And five guys with giant umbrellas jumped all over poor Kristen to make sure nobody could see it."

Bannerman recalled that the helicopter kept to the altitude required by aviation regulations. At the time, he was sure nothing could be

Bella's parents, Charlie (Billy Burke) and Renée (Sarah Clarke), give her a special gift on her wedding day: a jeweled hair comb.

Bella's stepfather, Phil Dwyer (Ty Olsson), makes his first appearance in the films, with Renée and Charlie.

"In designing the wedding, I tried to get inside Alice's head and think about her inspirations and influences, since she's witnessed over one hundred years of fashion and cultural references. Ashley [Greene] and I liked the idea that Alice was a fan of classic movies that embodied nostalgic elegance. We looked at the dresses Ginger Rogers wore and combined those influences with a contemporary aesthetic. From there I started sketching. For Alice herself, Ashley and I fell in love with the idea of a short, flapper-style dress with 1930s-style iridescent beading and ostrich-feather detailing—something that would move beautifully on the dance floor!"

—MICHAEL WILKINSON, COSTUME DESIGNER

Alice (Greene) shows off her vintage-inspired fashion.

seen under the wisteria-blossom canopy, a suspicion that was confirmed when he later went up in a helicopter to shoot aerial footage of the Cullen house and the forest. "You couldn't see anything; we had it pretty contained by the vegetation and the dynamics of the set. The house does stick out, but we were constantly under tree cover in the thick of the woods."

Eventually, the helicopter left, and the wedding was on. Bill Condon describes the journey of Bella's walk down the aisle. "We showed it from Bella's point of view, the viewpoint of this incredibly strong-willed but, paradoxically, anxious person running a gauntlet of people, a person who did not want to be the center of attention you have to be as a bride. But there's Edward, waiting, and there's your love and trust in him to get you there. That scene is the perfect example of our immersion approach. It's not like watching the recent royal wedding on television—it's like you're right up there with them."

During the early outline- and screenplay-writing stage, the director wanted to avoid "blocks of exposition"—and such was the introduction of the Denali sisters, notably Irina (played by Maggie Grace), whose full story would be told in the second movie. "In early drafts for the second movie, we had to explain their whole backstory, and it seemed awkward," Condon recalled. "By having them at the wedding, we could watch their behavior instead of explaining everything in a flashback [for the second movie]."

"THEY HAD TO WALK IN AND BE DROP-DEAD GORGEOUS."

In the novel, before the Denali sisters converted to "vegetarian" vampirism, they were temptresses whose sexual conquests usually ended in blood. Hair, makeup, and costume worked together for the Irina, Kate, and Tanya characters. "They had to walk in and be drop-dead gorgeous," said Michael Wilkinson. "This was Bill's and my thing, that even though their amazing beauty makes everyone stop and stare, you had to believe these people could walk through the world as we know it and not be front-page news! By the choice of silhouettes, necklines, and fabrics, I made sure they looked great as a team, but also had variations for their characters."

"The Denali sisters had distinct looks based on their characters," hairstylist Rita Parillo added. "Kate is described in the story as having hair like corn silk, which we tried to imitate by putting a hair-straightening product on Casey LaBow's hair, and using a flatiron to help maintain the silky look. Tanya, played by MyAnna Buring, is seen at the wedding with a sexy 'goddess' up-do, and later we had her with a more loose and wavy style, which suited the feistiness of the character. For Irina, Maggie Grace wore a soft do, but [in *Part 1*] she does have her hair down. The blond trio looked excellent together, yet each character's look stood alone."

"The makeup team worked hard to create a flow between humans and vampires," added makeup head Jean Black. "The idea going in was 'young and romantic,' so we tried to stay true to that."

Esme (Reaser) chats with the Denali sisters, from left: Irina (Maggie Grace), Kate (Casey LaBow), and Tanya (MyAnna Buring).

In another key scene, Jacob has a quiet moment alone with Bella and expresses shock that she wants a *real* honeymoon. "We've had three movies of Edward and Jacob's conflict, and Jacob's jealousy and all of that," Rosenberg said. "We were worried it might start getting repetitive, with Jacob breaking into yet another rage over Edward and Bella's relationship. We wanted to handle that scene at the wedding in a way that advanced the story and their relationship. We basically dialed down Jacob's outburst. The point of the scene is to convey to the audience, and to remind Bella, that what she wants could kill her."

During filming of the reception, the rain returned. "The idea for the reception in the forest was very beautiful and organic," Navarro added. "We wanted to make all these things belong there, [show] that it was real nature and not a set. The problem was fighting the rain. We had to have flying frames and fabrics to contain it; we had to move the actors

in and out and dump the excess water."

"There was a bit of a rain canopy set up, but it was raining so hard on both nights that every now and then water would pour out of this canopy in a waterfall effect," Jan Blackie-Goodine recalled. "It was difficult for the actors—you could see their breath, it was so cold. After the first night, my crew had to come in early in the morning and strip off all the table decorations and the napkins, and take them to an industrial Laundromat in Squamish. Then we had to come back and re-dress the set. As we were dressing it, we were tenting all the tables with plastic to keep them dry until they were ready for filming, because it had been raining all day."

"There were water and mud up to the ankles [at the reception]," Sherman recalled. "The weather was so against us. But for the wedding ceremony, the sun came out. We got Kristen down all the way from the house to the wedding area, then down the aisle. It all worked."

"Bella's absolutely certain that she wants to spend forever with Edward, but there's something about marriage that she's apprehensive about, and it comes from the way she was brought up. There are a few beats right before the wedding actually occurs that really send her into the anxiety that she brings into the ceremony as she first starts walking down the aisle."

—KRISTEN STEWART, ACTRESS

Bella, before (above) and after the wedding vows.

*Alice (Ashley Greene),
Jasper (Jackson Rathbone),
Esme (Elizabeth Reaser), and
Carlisle (Peter Facinelli)
wait for the bride.*

"When Kristen walked down the aisle, it was very moving. When Bella looks into Edward's eyes, you can see three years of moviemaking and storytelling building up into a sequence where not a word is spoken. When fans see this scene, they'll understand how real and delicate Bella and Edward's relationship is, and how exhilarating it is to be a part of it."

—BILL BANNERMAN, CO-PRODUCER AND AERIAL UNIT DIRECTOR

Bella and Edward

Bella and Edward's wedding attracted the interest of a variety of high-profile fashion designers. In the final film, contributions came from Brioni, which worked on the men's suits, and Carolina Herrera, who was involved in creating the much-anticipated wedding dress. The costume designer evoked a mix of contemporary and vintage design, including 1930s Hollywood, that dazzling era of men in top hats and tails, and women in glittering evening gowns.

Lorin Flemming and Mike Sabo coordinated with the jewelry designer so that Lorin's invitation flourish and Bella's hair comb and ring were all in the same Victorian style. The hair comb was created by The Gilded Lily.

"Bella's shoes were custom designed by Manolo Blahnik for the film. They took their classic eggshell satin pump and added a beautiful and unique motif—an embroidered flower that crosses from the toe toward the ankle. It is a wonderful sculptural element that makes the shoes instantly recognizable, and is both romantic and fashion-forward."

—MICHAEL WILKINSON, COSTUME DESIGNER

64

"When Stephenie, Bill, and I talked about the wedding dress, we wanted it to have a vintage feel, and at the same time capture a sense of young love. Its originality and elegance would come from its simplicity, which would let Kristen's beauty shine. In collaborating with the designers at Carolina Herrera, we considered many versions, until we came upon the final one. We loved the strength of the open back filled with a sheer layer of French lace, and the bold simplicity of the front. We knew this would give the dress an instantly recognizable quality appropriate for such an iconic costume."

—MICHAEL WILKINSON, COSTUME DESIGNER

Bella saves a dance for Jacob.

65

Bella and Edward

"The dress has very unique, sinuous seams running down the front, with panels of parallel stitching at the waist, dozens of tiny silk-covered buttons down the center back and at the cuffs, and a flared train. All of these details bring to mind the corseted hourglass dresses of the Edwardian era. Yet, the choice of a supple silk satin, cut on the cross-grain, with no structured under-pinnings, makes the dress seem contemporary and fresh. The scooped neck-line is demure, the sleeves are long, the skirt is to the ground, and yet the thin double layer of satin reveals every line of Kristen's amazing physique. The result is a perfect combination of modest and modern."

—MICHAEL WILKINSON, COSTUME DESIGNER

"Brioni is a venerable Italian label that has been cutting beautiful suits for discerning gentlemen around the world for decades—we thought they were the perfect collaborator for the men's suits for the wedding party. I spent a lot of time getting my designs together and sketching up my ideas. I knew I wanted the suits to have some elegant vintage details but also be modern and youthful. I sent my sketches to the Brioni studio in Milan, along with some period tailoring references. They sent back flawlessly constructed suits that fit our cast beautifully."

—MICHAEL WILKINSON, COSTUME DESIGNER

A Q&A with BREAKING DAWN author Stephenie Meyer

How does it feel to walk around a film set that takes a location from your imagination and realizes it in physical form?

STEPHENIE MEYER: It can feel very surreal to be on set, especially when it matches up closely to what I've imagined. On *Breaking Dawn*, we built the Cullen house in a forest for the first time; before that, it had existed only in pieces on soundstages. The surroundings were so beautiful, and the river especially was very similar to what I'd seen in my head. Standing out by the river with the house behind me felt strange, like something I might wake up from.

The film adaptations have attempted to be faithful to the novels, and you have been involved in each film. What have you learned about the medium of movies and, in comparison, the art of writing?

SM: Creating a movie is all about compromise. There are budgetary constraints, physical constraints, and time constraints. You may end up shooting London in downtown New Orleans, or Paris in a park in Baton Rouge. The actors don't have real superpowers, so you have to fake that as convincingly as possible. There are so many different visions of the same scene, and so the final version is an amalgam of all of them; it's never exactly what any one person envisioned.

Writing is so much easier on that front. It's all in your imagination, so the creative process has no compromise at all. You can easily make someone fly or transform or anything else you like without worrying about budgets or even physics. It's a quiet, focused process with just one vision. For me personally, it's a much purer kind of creation, and I find it more fulfilling. But creating movies is its own kind of fulfilling, and its own kind of fun. Both are experiences I enjoy.

It was a big decision whether to make BREAKING DAWN into one movie or two. What, ultimately, persuaded you that it should be two films?

SM: I was always open to either one or two movies—whichever told the story the best way. There were pros and cons to both versions. Melissa wrote up the treatment, and it seemed very, very long—easily two movies long. There were just a lot of plot elements to cover. Melissa felt like she could make two very solid scripts out of those elements, and I supported her vision. Having seen the first movie now, I am glad we decided to go in this direction. *Breaking Dawn Part 1* feels very full and suspenseful.

You had a cameo at the wedding, where you watched Bella finally walk down the aisle. What were your emotions on seeing your characters come to life for this pivotal event in THE TWILIGHT SAGA?

SM: It was a more emotional experience than I thought it would be. We didn't shoot the wedding until near the end of a very long process, but at the time I wasn't thinking about the finality of it all; I was just getting through it day by day. It was in the early days of the shoot that Bill [Condon] told us

Stephenie Meyer attends the wedding with Wyck Godfrey, Melissa Rosenberg, and Bill Bannerman.

his idea about having those of us who'd been involved since the first movie (me, Melissa Rosenberg, Wyck Godfrey, and Bill Bannerman) make an appearance at Bella's wedding. I thought he was joking. But then, months later, the time came and Michael Wilkinson [the costume designer] started asking me about wardrobe. The actuality of being an extra included two long, very cold days in thin summer clothes, sitting on damp wooden benches. I was glad to have my longtime friends sitting next to me, so we could huddle together for warmth, and come up with goofy stories about our characters to pass the time. (Wyck named his character Scotty McCreery—he was one of Charlie Swan's deputies. I was his wife, Stephenie McCreery—my first name having already been established in the *Twilight* diner—and we were having some domestic strife due to the fact that Scotty was in love with Charlie. Bill and Melissa were a couple as well: rich folks in from L.A. to see Melissa's old college roommate—Renée—be mother of the bride.)

So I wasn't thinking about my character [Bella]'s big moment until Kristen actually walked down the aisle, looking breathtaking in her dress. She seemed truly nervous. She looked at me for a second as she walked by on Billy Burke's arm, and that was when it hit me: We were wrapping it all up, and Bella and Edward weren't going to be a part of my daily life anymore. It felt a little bit sad, but also oddly triumphant to watch her walk by. I was so proud of

Kristen. She'd put so much work and passion into Bella's character, and it was kind of amazing to sit on the Swan side of the congregation and support her in her big moment. I did, in fact, tear up a little bit. It's one of my favorite memories from all the time I've spent on set.

The BREAKING DAWN novel doesn't so much end as it takes leave of the main characters. Have you thought of potential situations that Edward and Bella might face as a married couple? Can you envision returning to the Saga at some point, and picking up the story?

SM: When I was writing the TWILIGHT series, I was always thinking about the characters and what would happen to them. I had enough scenarios to cover the next century of their lives. I hope to write all those stories down someday, but if it happens, it won't be for a while. To be honest, I got a little burned out on vampires. When I was writing BREAKING DAWN, I could feel that I was going need to step away from these characters for a while, and I was not at all sure when I would come back to them. I made the decision to wrap things up with a happy ending so the readers wouldn't be left hanging indefinitely. But I couldn't make myself end the story in a way so final that I could never come back to it, just in case.

Honeymoon

Robert Pattinson and Kristen Stewart as
newlyweds Edward and Bella Cullen.

> "The real thing was trying to recapture the love between Bella and Edward and the journey toward the inevitable, which is her finally becoming a vampire and being with Edward forever. In terms of visual style, all of that is sensual, languid; there's a real beauty to it—there's not a lot of handheld camera chaos."

—WYCK GODFREY, PRODUCER

In BREAKING DAWN, the novel, Edward has long since gained control of his blood-lust around Bella. As their wedding day approaches he can kiss her lips, her throat, without fear of losing control, although he still feels the pang of longing. "He claimed he was long past the temptation my blood used to be for him, that the idea of losing me had cured him of any desire for it," Bella recalls on the eve of their wedding in the novel. "But I knew the smell of my blood still caused him pain—still burned his throat like he was inhaling flames."[8]

Having taken their vows, they are finally free to give themselves to each other. In the film, all of Bella's joy, fear, and longing are summed up in the car ride that begins their journey to the secret honeymoon retreat Edward has arranged.

As Bella watches the dark forest fly by, a clearing in the trees reveals an object that gets bigger and bigger—the gigantic *Cristo Redentor*, the "Christ the Redeemer" statue above Rio de Janeiro. "Bella and Edward are now on the way to their honeymoon and their intimacy as a married couple, and she has no idea where she's going," Bannerman explained. "Bill Condon wanted to condense the geographical reconfiguration via this kind of shot. So we had to do this intricate, choreographed move around the *Cristo* statue to marry with the shot [of Bella in the car]."

To shoot the plate, Bannerman went up in a lightweight AStar B2 helicopter with a Brazilian pilot. For this maneuver he couldn't even carry the operator who usually controlled the camera—the helicopter was heavy enough with

They filmed the car ride in front of a greenscreen.

two occupants and seven hundred pounds of mounted camera. They would also have to fly with minimal fuel to be light enough to battle the winds and perform their maneuver—the statue is one hundred thirty feet tall and stands atop a peak more than two thousand feet high. The setup included the typical aerodynamic sphere with a gyroscopic system holding a camera connected by cables and electronics to control panels in the cockpit, where an operator could make all the normal earthbound moves of pan and tilt, but also spin the camera.

The day of the shoot, cloud cover threatened to obscure the statue. "I need optimum weather for an aerial shoot," Bannerman explained, "but *Twilight* weather is a roll of the dice; we always have to find a balance between reasonably good and dismal weather. You need overcast, but you can't fly when there's a low cloud ceiling—conditions become too dangerous. If the statue was covered in clouds, we wouldn't be able to get the shot. We ferried up to Rio at midday, and by the time we started our daylight rehearsals at three in the afternoon, the clouds were just above the statue's head. We went out at dusk and magic-hour light. We started shooting and got it! I headed off to do more work in downtown Rio. Twenty minutes later, I looked back at the statue—it was completely engulfed in clouds. The weather *and* movie gods smiled on us that day."

The filming in Brazil opened principal photography. As in the novel, the actors would get into a boat docked in Rio to set sail for Isle Esme, the private island named for the matriarch of the Cullen coven.

On location in Brazil.

"It's my job as an aerial director to find the nuances of the story and give the director different options. He might want a fluid shot over the rooftop versus a dive-bomber move that speaks of something completely different. It's easy to do establishing shots, but challenging to take it to the next level of creating a magical environment. I would achieve that by composition and fluid camera moves, finding a vampire-esque, or romantic, way—drifting like a leaf blowing in the wind. I used that analogy with my pilot. It wasn't a mechanical move from Point A to Point B. You choreograph to reflect the mood."

—BILL BANNERMAN,
CO-PRODUCER AND AERIAL UNIT DIRECTOR

Edward and Bella take a high-speed boat ride to their honeymoon hideaway.

The romantic nighttime boat ride was shot off the coast of Rio, in Paraty, which had a channel with a natural wind tunnel the aerial work took into account. The arrival at the island was a classic "day for night" shot. "It's impossible to light the ocean at night, so we shot during the day at low light levels," said Bannerman. "I used the reflection of the sun in the water as moonlight, another standard cheat."

"I've done all the aerials since I came aboard on *New Moon*," Bannerman added. "I've done aerials on a lot of shows; it's a passion of mine. I direct all the work that has to be done from an aerial perspective, anything not accomplished from a camera crane, whether chasing a boat, a Porsche, or a motorcycle, or filming establishing shots of sunrises and sunsets. There's a multitude of elements required from the air, including storytelling points and working in conjunction with choreographed elements on the ground. An example was filming a boat driven on open water by two stunt doubles when we have our heroes going to Isle Esme. You have to consider so many elements. When you watch the actors leave a wharf in Rio de Janeiro, then what? How do they get to the island, how fast, how much time does it take?"

In preproduction, the island and house where Bella and Edward spend their honeymoon generated considerable back-and-forth. It was finally decided to shoot the exteriors in Brazil and match the architectural style of the location house with an interior set in Baton Rouge. Prior to principal photography, the search for the production's own Isle Esme began off the coast of Rio.

"[Finding] the beach house was a real nightmare," recalled Richard Sherman, who assembled an art department in Brazil. One challenge was the reality of Brazil. "A lot of great ideas got thrown out because once you get down to Brazil you see it's not a beach community like the Hamptons or Malibu, with big estates. It's very low-key. Even the rich have beach houses that are open, with thatched roofs and posts

The couple went casual for their tropical getaway.

"Bill and I were excited about the honeymoon as the classic American summer vacation, almost like JFK and Jackie at Martha's Vineyard. We wanted it to be fresh and romantic and young, for the audience to delight in seeing Bella finally out of her flannel shirts and into clothes Alice had chosen for her. Bella struggles with this new image of herself, not feeling quite herself in the ladylike dress Alice packed for the arrival in Rio; the mortifying lingerie; and the cute, sweet, white bikini. As the holiday goes on, we had fun exploring how Bella starts to relax and add her own inevitable style. She wears some of Edward's shirts and starts throwing clothing together, maybe not the way Alice intended, but in a more spontaneous, Bella-like fashion."

—MICHAEL WILKINSON,
COSTUME DESIGNER

and open-air kitchens, and big, beautiful beds covered with gauze."

The novel imagined a romantic, lonely island, but Brazil's coastline is dotted with hundreds of small islands near to one another. "Remote islands just don't exist down there," Sherman noted. "There's also a lot of politics in Brazil. We found a great house we wanted to use, but it turned out it was a point of contention with the government because it was built illegally and on the list of houses to be blown up. I had to get on a plane and fly down to Rio to look for a new house."

For the next month, Sherman and his Brazilian art department sailed the coastline in a huge boat, searching for the right house on an island. The production designer's hospitable hosts introduced him to a wide range of experiences, everything from Rio's lively underground bossa nova clubs to a memorable lunch where they switched from their big boat to a smaller boat that carried them to a rocky isle with a restaurant, complete with waiters and fish sizzling on a grill. Workdays were filled with sun, sailing, and the sights of deserted islands with tropical foliage and dense jungle. "About the third day, I asked myself, 'Am I getting paid for this?' It was like a vacation," Sherman said with a smile.

The expedition finally found what they were looking for: an island with a house in

> FOR THE NEXT MONTH, SHERMAN AND HIS BRAZILIAN ART DEPARTMENT SAILED THE COASTLINE IN A HUGE BOAT, SEARCHING FOR THE RIGHT HOUSE ON AN ISLAND.

waters dotted with five or six other isles (during early postproduction, Sherman explained that the plan was to digitally erase one to provide a clearer view of their Isle Esme). Although aspects of the location were ideal, there were problems. "We liked the location and interior of the house, but the outside wasn't great," Sherman noted. "It was on a grassy knoll, so we had to create a beach. Our house has a roof and walls, but there are open areas. The doors don't slide; they pivot and swing open. The back wall opens to the jungle, and the front wall opens to the sea, so you're sitting on a beach, basically, with nothing around you. That's how they live down there."

Sherman and his Brazilian crew spent the next three weeks getting the house ready for the arrival of Condon, Navarro, and the rest of the first unit. "One day, we're working and this [police officer] comes by in a boat and says, 'We just want to let you know that at three o'clock today there's going to be a big explosion—we're blowing up the house next door.' We couldn't see the house because it was around the next inlet, but three o'clock rolls around and—*BOOM!*—they blew up the house next door! Our whole house shook; we saw these plumes of black smoke. And then the jungle caught on fire, and the fire brigade had to come to put out the fire so our place wouldn't burn down. So, there were adult moments."

Edward (Pattinson) and Bella (Stewart) play chess in a nod to the novel's cover, and to stay dry during tropical rainstorms. Above and below, the set of the honeymoon house on Isle Esme.

The couple went for a night on the town, and the crew shot the scene on location in the hip Lapa district of Rio.

Throughout the scout and location prep, Sherman and his Brazilian crew enjoyed gorgeous weather. Finally, Condon and company arrived, slathered on sunscreen, and got ready to shoot. For a scene of Bella and Edward walking the streets of Rio, Sherman had suggested to Condon that they avoid tourist areas and shoot in a cool district where young people actually went: Rio's Lapa district. That was the first day's shoot, Sherman recalled.

As usual, the *Twilight* couple attracted a lot of attention on location. "There had been a couple movies to get used to the idea of the tension that location shooting creates among fans," Wilkinson noted. "In Brazil it bubbled a little bit out of control. There was a huge crowd outside when Robert and Kristen arrived at their hotel, and there were hundreds of people observing when we shot on the dock in Rio where they set out in the boat for the island."

The second day, the unit filmed a waterfall scene. On the third day, Sherman recalled, the first unit moved to the honeymoon island when the weather took a turn for the worse. "Suddenly, it turned into a tempest. It was practically a hurricane, with wind and black clouds and pouring rain. I left because I had to head back, but they couldn't leave the island. . . . The cast and crew had to sleep overnight in this house with no water, no food; they had to sleep on the ground."

"We managed to be there in the middle of a monsoon, basically," Condon recalled. "We never got lucky; it never got super sunny."

> ## AS USUAL, THE *Twilight* COUPLE ATTRACTED A LOT OF ATTENTION ON LOCATION.

Richard Sherman called it a miss—because of stormy and overcast skies, the first unit never quite got the azure blue of the island waters, or the beach's creamy-white sands. Still, the director felt satisfied that they'd gotten what they came for—except for a key scene of Bella and Edward's moonlit swim, when they first make love. The first unit would make that up at the end of the schedule; in the meantime, there was plenty of honeymoon business to attend to when they returned to Baton Rouge. The interior work began with the honeymoon house, another greenscreen set that would incorporate location plates shot by a visual effects unit headed by Terry Windell.

The marriage bed was realized as a classic draped four-poster bed. It embodied set decorator David Schlesinger's perspective on the movie's general design: "A modern take on traditional things."

"A four-poster bed is a very Victorian kind of idea, but there are modern four-poster beds, and that's what we ended up with," Schlesinger added. "It's a simple teakwood bed. In the end, we looked at about twenty different beds before we decided on the one that we used."

Two teakwood beds were purchased. One was designed and engineered to show the aftermath of the couple's first experience. "The honeymoon is the first time they have sex, and we had to figure out how to show the damage to the bed, the feathers [from ripped-open pillows], all that crazy stuff," said art director Flemming. "Finding the right bed, and figuring out how to

The beautiful
waterfall near
Paraty, Brazil.

make parts break away but be safe for the actors, was a collaboration between Richard, David, the director, and myself. That's the part of my job that's really fun—figuring out little problems like that."

Working to the art department's specifications, the special effects team, headed by Alex Burdett, rigged one of the beds with breakaway bits that could fall apart without endangering the actors. "It's choreography, basically," Flemming observed. "Several pieces of the top frame get broken down, the sheets around the canopy are shredded, one of the posts is broken, the headboard is split in half because Edward is gripping it so hard and trying not to hurt her with his vampire strength—the women in the audience are just going to go crazy!"

In the novel, Edward's greatest fear is realized when he sees the bruises Bella has the next morning. But their lovemaking also has a more unexpected result that shocks Edward into a near catatonic state.

"Stephenie delicately explains Bella's pregnancy in her mythology, but you just go with it," Rosenberg noted. "Every now and then, I'll look at an Internet fan site and someone will refer to something about Edward as, 'It's a fact.' Fact? He's a fictional character! But there's such an attachment to the mythology of vampires. So, if vampires can exist, why not vampire sperm?"

The shocking revelation sends Bella and Edward rushing home, and sets the rest of the story in motion.

Two teak beds were purchased. The honeymoon suite before . . .

. . . and after. The bed was rigged to "fall apart."

"I think that you're never going to question if Edward and Bella are going to stay together, and it's never been that way. For me, that feels like the point that needs to really slam people."

—KRISTEN STEWART, ACTRESS

"The honeymoon is a very sensual section, and the culmination of the books. It's also where the conflict is more complex, with all the adult issues common in marriage, like sex and family. So it was important to carry forward the evolution of the honeymoon. We start with the nervousness. Then it's her wanting him and him not wanting her for fear of hurting her, to where she's seducing him and he's resisting before finally caving in. Bella is kind of awkward in that role as seductress, but the scene is about her getting control, and their enjoyment."

—MELISSA ROSENBERG, SCREENWRITER

HONEYMOON

Bella (Stewart) is at
Alice's mercy on the
honeymoon—she has
only the frilly clothes
her new sister-in-law
packed for her!

*Edward (Pattinson) carries in
all the luggage his sister packed.*

Edward gallantly carries his bride across the threshold.

"Brazil was kind of chaotic, and it was very beautiful. The first couple of days we were there were amazing; [it was] the most amazing environment. And then almost everything that could go wrong went wrong. We were in hurricane-force winds and monsoon rains... [and we were] supposed to be having an ideal honeymoon!"

—ROBERT PATTINSON, ACTOR

*The happy couple
can finally relax.*

The couple who clean the honeymoon getaway, Gustavo and Kaure (played by Sebastião Lemos and Carolina Virguez), suspect Edward is up to no good.

The morning after, Bella has a glow about her.

90

Bella (Stewart) consults the Cullens on the new development as Edward (Pattinson) looks on anxiously.

Wolf People

The Quileute wolf pack: Chaske Spencer as Sam, Alex Meraz as Paul, Bronson Pelletier as Jared, Kiowa Gordon as Embry, Tyson Houseman as Quil, Braydon Jimmie as Collin, and Swowo Gabriel as Brady.

> "We called them the Wolf People—Phil Tippett and his company."
>
> —SCOTT ATEAH, STUNT COORDINATOR

In the books and films, the shape-shifting wolves of the Quileute tribe prowl their territory while maintaining an uneasy truce with the Cullen coven. In fact, the wolves abide in a multiuse residential and light industrial section of Berkeley, California—specifically, in the digital realm of the Tippett Studio's computers. With the computer-animated wolves, the animation and visual effects house had a rare opportunity to evolve their work throughout the films. "In some ways, you're learning about the characters like actors do," Phil Tippett noted. "You're building who these characters are; you find new ways of presenting them and playing their psychological side."

Tippett Studio's research included a wolf pelt that had been on hand since preproduction on *The Twilight Saga: New Moon*. It had recently been put up on the wall of the studio's art department, its layered fur with its distinct colorations and markings a constant reminder of the goal for effects artists seeking to replicate reality. "We're getting there, but we're still far from being able to render the amount of fur a real animal has, and a wolf's thick and distinctive coat, and the way it mats a certain way," mused art director Nate Fredenburg, whose open office space has a clear view of the wolf

pelt. "It's been nice to be able to evolve a character; it's rare. We've had primarily the same team of people on all the films. What we discovered early on, in *New Moon*, was there weren't a lot of variations we could put in the wolves that mattered. We had scale and proportion differences, a lot of stuff that didn't really read on-screen. What *does* read is color, and that's what we focused on—getting distinct color markings for each wolf."

Throughout the series, including the *Breaking Dawn* films, the Jacob wolf was the "hero" model for all the wolves. On *New Moon*, Tippett began with four wolves, led by Jacob's shape-shifting incarnation. By *Eclipse* there were eight: Alpha male Sam, Jacob, Seth, Quil, Leah, Paul, Embry, and Jared. Along the way, the wolves evolved according to the aesthetic preference of each director. "Chris Weitz had the idea of the wolves as sentinels standing proud and tall, and you do see wolves in those poses," Tippett producer Ken Kokka said. "You also see them with their heads down, in a skulking, menacing mode, and David Slade preferred that."

"Bill was fine with the way the wolves worked," added Tippett, who shared his shop's visual effects supervising duties with Eric Leven. "His main concern was he felt the wolves were a

> "From *New Moon* we pretty much went straight into production on *Eclipse*. But we had enough time between *Eclipse* and *Breaking Dawn* to say, 'Okay, let's rebuild the Jacob wolf and make him better.'"
>
> —KEN KOKKA, VISUAL EFFECTS PRODUCER, TIPPETT STUDIO

"As an audience, and even for me, to watch Jacob transform like this is cool, but it's weird because you know Jacob starts out the movie as this young teenager liking this girl that he can't get, and throughout the movie he splits from his pack. He realizes that this is not what's supposed to happen, and he has to become a man and do the right thing."

—TAYLOR LAUTNER,
ACTOR

Jared, Jacob, and Seth.

Jacob.

"The Alpha male issue comes up, the tribe is there, the wolves are circling, and Jacob wants to protect Bella against the wishes of the Alpha, Sam. We imagined how to do the dialogue: Do we play it fast or slow? What is the intensity level? Also, who looks at whom determines shot length and is a guide for us to build around."

—**PHIL TIPPETT**, VISUAL EFFECTS
SUPERVISOR, TIPPETT STUDIO

Sam and Jacob face off as Leah and Paul watch.

> "This is the movie where Jacob becomes an Alpha wolf. We show a little bit of the changing of the guard, that Jacob is now stepping into his birthright."
>
> —**TOM GIBBONS**, ANIMATION SUPERVISOR, TIPPETT STUDIO

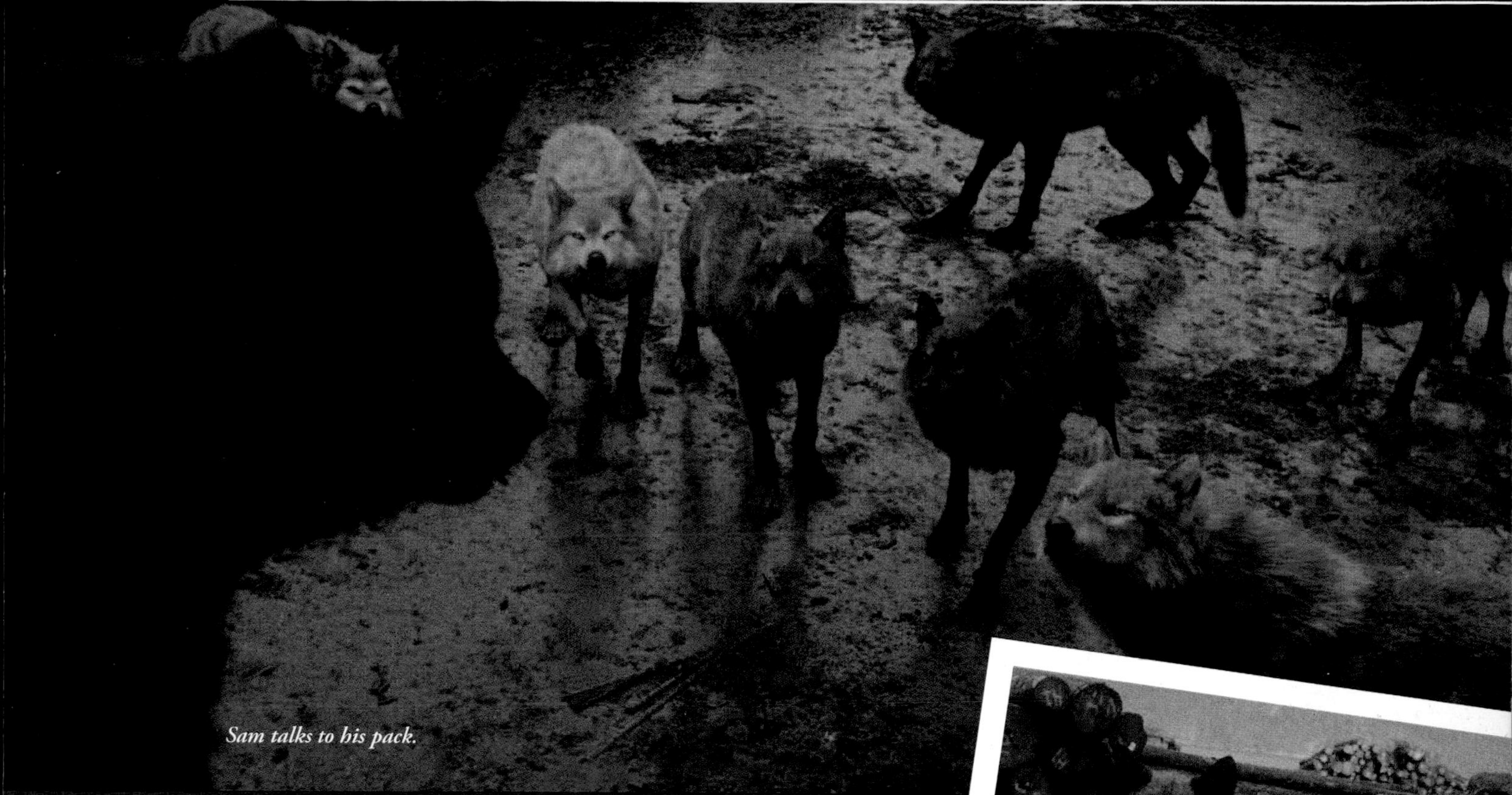

Sam talks to his pack.

Jacob and Seth.

Jacob fights with Leah.

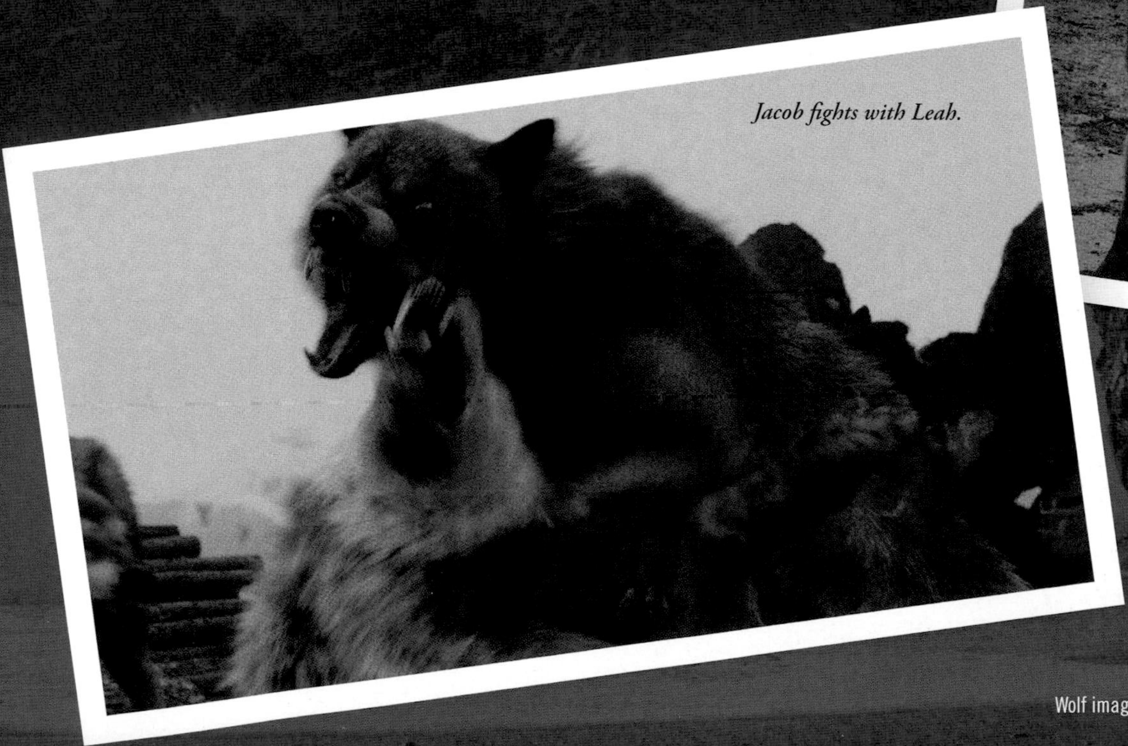

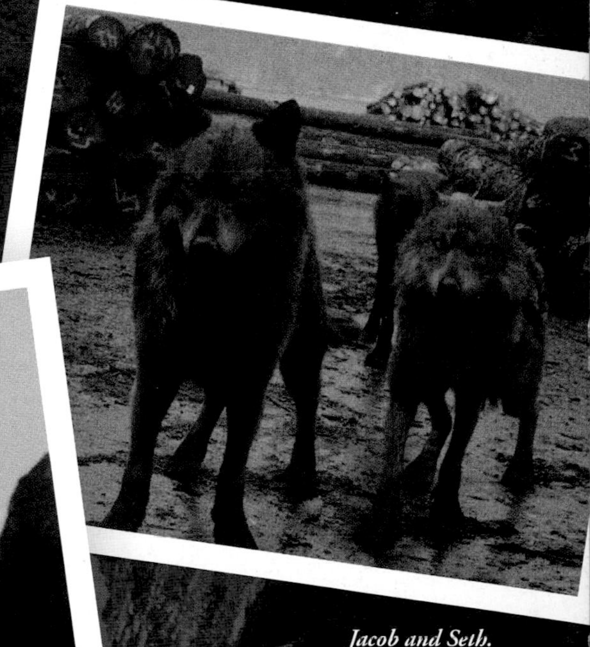

little too big, so we scaled them down, although nothing too noticeable. But whatever show we're working on, we have to readjust to the requirements of the script. The real issue for us was that we have ten wolves for *Breaking Dawn Part 1*, and sixteen for *Part 2*—in computer graphics terms, that takes hours and hours to render. A lot of R&D went into rejiggering the wolves so they looked the same but were faster to render."

Fredenburg's role on all the *Twilight Saga* films was the "look end." There had been technological leaps on *New Moon* and *Eclipse*, but *Breaking Dawn* went beyond those benchmarks. "We've been able to leverage the work for a third evolutionary step," Fredenburg explained. "We had to simultaneously tackle aesthetics and the efficiency of rendering. We ended up able to render sixteen wolves that had, roughly, ten million hairs each in the same time we rendered eight on the last show. As a side effect, we created a few more tools to give us a better aesthetic."

The high-resolution 3-D modeling process

> "A LOT OF R&D WENT INTO REJIGGERING THE WOLVES SO THEY LOOKED THE SAME BUT WERE FASTER TO RENDER."

included "guide spline curves" that told the proprietary fur tool everything it needed to know about the fur and how to interpolate it—where to put it, its shape, its length, and its angle. The efficiency was felt at the lighting stage, Fredenburg explained. "The animator's scenes get handed to our lighting TDs [technical directors], who also take the work the painters do and add lights and fold that into their render jobs before it goes to compositing. All the efficiencies we built upstream got realized when they started lighting and rendering. We spent less time calculating the hairs."

Tippett Studio began "creeping into the show" in August 2010, producer Kokka recalls. Supervisors Tippett and Leven didn't have to be at the Baton Rouge soundstages, where they spent several months working on a greenscreen stage for a big sequence for the second movie, until after Christmas. Then they moved on to the forest location outside Squamish for two major scenes for the first film: one a gathering of the wolf pack that required heavy dialogue, the other the climactic battle between wolves and vampires. The location work included shooting background plates and collecting precise measurements to accurately place the CG wolves within the live-action environments. The process began in the conceptual stage of hand-drawn storyboards and low-resolution computer graphics. "We were pre-vizing as they started shooting; it was almost a race," Kokka recalled.

"Eric [Leven] would call us from the set and say, 'Give us another take; we need three more wolves,'" added Tippett film editor Mike Cavanaugh. "We were working as they were shooting in Baton Rouge. With the Cullen fight we were only a day ahead of shooting. But with Scene 92, we really set the pace."

Scene 92, also called the "the lumberyard sequence," was the pivotal scene where the wolves gather to hear Alpha leader Sam (played by Chaske Spencer) announce that Bella is pregnant and that her child poses a risk to the tribe, so they cannot let it live. Jacob boldly defies Sam, breaks from the pack, and heads to the Cullen house, where he will help watch over Bella. As in the novels, and for the first time in the films, the wolves "speak" telepathically. Although Tippett always created the wolves to be as realistic as possible (albeit larger and with dramatic license), here was a key story point where wolves had to perform and carry an entire scene.

"With Scene 92 it was possible to make that our show," Kokka added. "We pitched

Jacob (Lautner) pleads with Bella (Stewart).

99

it that we could board, pre-viz, and guide the shooting, which would save a lot of money. When you have a production willing to engage with you on that level, you're in luck. Our creative team felt invested from the beginning; we felt less like a vendor and more like a group of craftspeople collaborating. We could look at this sequence and say, 'Yeah, we really helped build that!'"

"Everything was shooting in Canada at the same time, both first and second units," visual effects supervisor Bruno noted. "Bella and Charlie's house was like a hundred miles from the Cullen house in Squamish. I couldn't be everywhere, so it was like, 'Here's the storyboard, here's the pre-viz—go get this stuff!' From time to time, I'd see everyone's dailies, but Tippett had free rein to get his wolf stuff."

> "In the last movie we had Bella and Jacob [in wolf form] have a quiet moment, which was fun to do. Now we had a scene of Sam and Jacob in a power play, with dialogue, which was exciting. We worked through this scratch track where we did the dialogue first, and then the animatic. Mike [Cavanaugh] cut things different ways to figure out what worked better. Having that preproduction time, which is rare in this business, was invaluable."
>
> —ERIC LEVEN, VISUAL EFFECTS SUPERVISOR, TIPPETT STUDIO

The lumberyard scene began with the in-house boards drawn by Tippett animators Geoff Wheeler and William Elder-Groebe. The next step was creating the low-resolution 3-D animatic to put the sequence into motion. "Summit gave us a lot of leeway to experiment in different ways to do these wolves," said Cavanaugh. "Some of the storyboards looked almost Disney-esque, designed to convey emotion to the client, which we can't really get into the realistic wolves. The most exciting thing about cutting the sequence together was working with our animators to find the line between human acting and anthropomorphizing the animals."

The visuals themselves, in classic animation story-reel fashion, were driven by the scratch track voices. (A scratch track is a temporary audio recording used as a tool to map out animation and sync it up to the dialogue before the final audio is recorded.) Tippett called their temporary voice performances "a kind of Berkeley Repertory–Tippett Studio version of the script," and they were processed for an eerie telepathic effect. "We used our scratch track to build the dialogue and action, and worked with Bill in developing that," Tippett explained.

Courtesy of Tippett Studio

Charlie (Burke) knows Jacob is upset, but Sue Clearwater (Alex Rice) and Billy Black (Gil Birmingham) know what's really happening.

The first story reel was sent to Bill Condon in October 2010, and was a starting point for the next iteration scratch track that Condon directed with his actors on location. That first animatic helped Tippett further refine the shots based on the director's notes and, once final changes were approved, provided "a working template for the shot itself," Kokka explained. "Devin Breese, our surveyor, went up with Phil and did full three-sixties at the location, and photos of the set. We sent them our pre-viz with our wolves on green and they were able to key in, or superimpose, our low-res wolves into the background plates. It enabled the guys to set up the shots really quickly in [Squamish]. We shot the entire sequence in a day and a half."

"Our pre-viz was not just grounded in performance and acting, but the real, practical decisions, such as the camera position," Leven explained. "When we got there on the day, it looked exactly like what we'd set up in 3-D. We knew exactly where the camera was going to be, the whole works."

The location for the background plates was a logging camp near Squamish, south of where the Cullen house and wedding were shot. "It was right where water from the ocean comes inland," Tippett described. "It was like fjord country."

What the Tippett team referred to as the "amphitheater" required stacks of logs to provide a dramatic space and story points, such as the logs forming a podium for Sam's address to the group. Tippett's on-set team worked with

Sue Clearwater (Alex Rice) and
Billy Black (Gil Birmingham).

second-unit director E. J. Foerster and second-unit DP Roger Vernon, who provided what Leven called "really good notes" that pushed for the dramatic effect of making the live-action space enclosed, like a wolf's lair.

"I went out with Roger Vernon and E. J. Foerster to all the locations to spec them out," Tippett said. "They had already been okayed by Bill and Guillermo; now we had to figure out how to use them. In terms of the logging-camp scene, we had a pretty significant hand in art decorating and designing the whole thing. We had to set up this amphitheater, so Eric built a 3-D set of the logging camp so he, Roger Vernon, and I had the location's geographical coordinates. We built a virtual configuration of these stacks of logs and ran that through the [main] art department. Roger and

E. J. and I figured out where the sun was, what the backgrounds were, what was the best way to point the camera to get the best visual."

The day of the big "log sort," Tippett visited the lumber camp on his lunch break to check out the work. "We'd hired the boss, who had these gigantic machines that look like prehistoric monsters, and he used them to carry and stack these gigantic logs. This guy was amazing. He was placing the logs in a specific configuration, laying everything out like an artist would lay out his color scheme for a painting. There were also a lot of safety concerns. You get cylindrical pieces of wood that weigh a couple tons stacked on top of each other, they can come tumbling down if you aren't careful about how you pin and cable them down."

On the animation side, Tippett supervisor

Tom Gibbons has had wolves on the brain for three years of *The Twilight Saga* productions—he even found himself doodling wolves in his notebooks during lulls in tech-heavy meetings. "I get to become a savant on every creature I work on, and every *Twilight* movie I come across some compelling information about wolves. On *Breaking Dawn Part 1*, the newest nugget I discovered was the notion that, eons ago, primitive tribes and ancient societies associated shape-shifting with wolves. They believed wolves could transform themselves into other things to get close to humans, or they could infuse humans with the ability to shape-shift.

"We, as animators, pull from a wide breadth of material and, as we get closer to the film, those avenues narrow to what we can get in a shot. Also, we always have to remember it has to be theatrical—it's not a documentary. But it doesn't make the process any less fun, and we bring some of that information to a shot. The way THE TWILIGHT SAGA novels and screenplays are written, and the way the actors portray the wolves, is what you'd find in a real wolf society."

The animators had been amassing knowl-

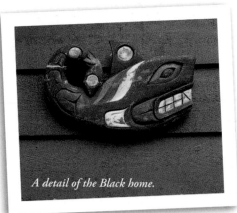

A detail of the Black home.

edge of wolf behavior since their first visit to a wolf sanctuary for *The Twilight Saga: New Moon*. The power struggle between Sam and Jacob tapped into the hierarchical caste system wolves are born into, with Alpha males at the top, followed by Betas and Omegas. "The Alphas have their distinct behavior, such as the way they hold their ears upright; they rarely flatten them in anger," Gibbons explained. "Alphas may not be the biggest or tallest in the pack, but they usually stand taller than anyone else. Ironically, Betas are usually the bigger wolves. Paul is our Beta wolf, the aggressor in the pack, a tougher kid and one of the larger wolves.

"You're a born Alpha, Beta, or Omega. Many wolf packs have two or more Alphas. When there is more than one Alpha, the other acts as a Beta until it's strong, big, and old enough to take the Alpha's position. The wolf-pack society is such a closed society that they rarely kick out a wolf. When that displacement happens, the older Alpha finds a new position in the pack. We find that happening in *Breaking Dawn*, with the conflict between Jacob and Sam."

"In the wolf acting we introduced the idea of telepathic exchanges. The challenge was how to support the dialogue with interesting performance. What was nice was our animators were able to introduce wolf behavior, such as hierarchical behavior of dominance and submission when Sam faces off against Jacob."

—NATE FREDENBURG, ART DIRECTOR, TIPPETT STUDIO

Jacob's world: Way Beach on Vancouver Island stands in for La Push. Top row from left: Alex Meraz as Paul; Taylor Lautner as Jacob; Kiowa Gordon as Embry and Booboo Stewart as Seth; Bronson Pelletier as Jared; Julia Jones as Leah. Bottom row, from left: Braydon Jimmie as Collin and Swowo Gabriel as Brady; Tinsel Korey as Emily with Chaske Spencer as Sam; Jared and Kim; Paul with Tanaya Beatty as Rachel.

The Birth

Kristen Stewart as expectant mother Bella Cullen.

"I got a lot of questions about how I was going to convey the birthing scene, because it's so bloody and graphic in the book. I never had a problem telling the birth from Bella's perspective because almost everything in the books is from Bella's perspective. But some fans were up in arms that we'd make a movie that wasn't R rated, because they wanted to see the blood. After years of working on *Dexter*, I know it's better to *not* see, but suggest, graphic brutality—it becomes more terrifying in your imagination. The essential part of that scene is Bella's terror, and the terror of everyone in that room, and that's what I focused on. Blood is not that important to really convey the terror of the scene."

—MELISSA ROSENBERG, SCREENWRITER

If one were hiking through the forest outside Forks and came upon a certain house in the woods, the first reaction might be astonishment that such a huge house would be there, half-hidden in the wilds. Coming from the back of the house, one would see stairs leading from the forest floor to a patio. Through the back, French doors open onto a lavish office and study—the private sanctum of Dr. Carlisle Cullen. It is here that Bella Swan, dying from her unnatural pregnancy, will labor to deliver her unique child.

In the screenwriting stage, Rosenberg had doubts about the potential first film, largely based on Bella's predicament: "How do you make a visually compelling movie about someone who is lying there, dying of a pregnancy? It's gruesome, depressing, and *static*, something that would work for a theatrical play. I had to find how to make it visually compelling. I resolved that in the structuring of the first movie. Act One is the wedding; Act Two, Part One, is the honeymoon; Act Two, Part Two, is the pregnancy; Act Three is the birth. There are essentially four acts, at thirty screenplay pages each, more or less. The pregnancy is one-fourth of the movie, and the birth itself is very dynamic. I realized the part where she's lying

Carlisle (Facinelli) waits with Bella (Stewart).

Below, Edward (Pattinson) confides in Carlisle (Peter Facinelli) his guilt over his bloody past and his fears for Bella.

Many interior scenes were shot on a soundstage with green-screens outside the windows.

Jacob (Lautner) keeps Bella warm.

around pregnant and dying is a nice chunk of the story, but doesn't dominate."

The accelerated pregnancy, with the human/vampire child growing inside, denying Bella nutrients and slowly killing her, was another equation to be solved through collaboration, from the director and cinematographer to costume, hair, makeup, special and visual effects, the art department, and construction crews.

The birthing included a new dynamic at the Cullen household—Jacob, Seth, and Leah, who come to keep vigil and guard Bella during her ordeal. "Jacob spends so much time at the Cullen house, and since he no longer has access to his own environment, there's the implication that Esme gives him clothes from the Cullen household," Wilkinson said. "We didn't necessarily want to represent that too strongly. It would give the wrong idea if Jacob started walking around in beautiful Edward-style shirts. Jacob never really finds peace with the Cullens' world. We wanted to show his discomfort, his feeling a little like a fish out of water."

The birthing was filmed on the Baton Rouge Cullen house set in January, while the aftermath, with Sam and his wolf pack arriving to kill the newborn, was shot outside the Cullen house set in Squamish in late April. The dizzying logistics had to be anticipated during preproduction the preceding summer. "There were a multitude of different and complex meth-

At left, Edward finally "hears" the baby and reconnects with Bella. Below, Rosalie's past makes her the baby's staunchest supporter.

odologies in executing Bella's birthing, to sell the creative beats," Bannerman noted. "What happens to Bella's body? How does she become so emaciated it looks like the process is threatening her life? How do you do that, or even address the idea of a vampire/human baby being born? You know fans will scrutinize this sequence and you have to deliver, excuse the pun, so the audience is caught up in the event, not its technical execution."

Helping Kristen Stewart make that transformation was John Rosengrant of Legacy Effects, a new company that seeks to carry on the tradition of the late Stan Winston, whose studio produced animatronic creatures and makeup effects for such epic productions as the

> "YOU KNOW FANS WILL SCRUTINIZE THIS SEQUENCE AND YOU HAVE TO DELIVER, EXCUSE THE PUN."

Terminator, Predator, and Jurassic Park film series.[9] Rosengrant, a twenty-five-year veteran of Stan Winston Studio, whose recent Legacy credits include *Avatar*, noted that his field has increasingly moved toward "hybrid techniques" that meld practical with digital. Hybrid techniques were applied to Bella's birthing sequence, with Legacy providing makeup, prosthetics, and puppeteering that was digitally augmented by Lola Effects. "We had to come up with a look consistent with this baby sucking the life out of her, to sell this emaciated look," Rosengrant explained. "Everything was meant to be seamless and not draw attention to itself, to make it believable and to let Kristen's performance come through."

A life-size Bella stand-in was created to simulate her unnatural fall.

Stewart with her double.

The process began with Rosengrant showing visual effects supervisor Bruno reference photos. Disturbing early tests "freaked" some of the production principals, including the director, Bruno recalled. "I [reassured them] this was a process we controlled, an effect that could go as far, or as little, as needed."

Legacy was in discussions about working on *The Twilight Saga: Breaking Dawn* when suddenly, Rosengrant recalled, it was a go. Legacy took photos and scans of the actress, along with physical life castings of her face, hands, and feet for molds. But there were concerns about having enough time for only one makeup test. "The appliances had to be very carefully sculpted because they were blending off into the middle of her face, and that's hard for someone like Kristen, who has smooth, perfect skin," Rosengrant said. "All the edges and technical stuff had to be perfect to blend. We really wanted another test, but we learned so much from just the one test that we came in very knowledgeable on how to crack the code."

Arjen Tuiten sculpted the appliances and applied them, along with Brian Sipe. The prosthetic appliances showing Bella's progressive deterioration included a sunken collarbone and partial chest, a distended belly, and a cheekbone appliance. "Lola Effects could [digitally] push her cheeks in under the bone structure we added," Rosengrant explained.

The effects team came up with a calculated, three-stage progression for Bella's deterioration. The first was slightly gaunt, with noticeable weight loss. At the final stage Bella hits the limits of physical decay. "For the first stage there was a less pronounced collarbone prosthetic appliance," Rosengrant noted. "For the final stage, we used the pronounced collarbone and sunken chest piece; we put on the cheekbones, the collarbone, and the hand appliances."

The body scan was used to create a whole-body puppet version of the actress at her character's third stage of emaciation. "I'll never forget Kristen seeing the doll the first time it showed up," Condon recalled of the life-size figure. "Just imagine seeing a corpselike version of yourself! It was creepy."

"The full-body puppet freaked people out," Bruno recalled. "There's a scene where [Stewart] looks in the mirror and you see the bones sticking out on her ribcage and back, her collarbones and shoulder bones sticking out. What Lola did was scan the physical puppet and track that data onto Kristen, and then start manipulating the body, whittling it down."

The body puppet was made of solid silicon, with an adjustable part-aluminum armature, and was also used in a scene where an exhausted Bella collapses. "The character is supposed to fall hard to her knees, and Rob jumps in to grab her before she hits her head," Rosen-grant explained. "The collapse was old-school rod-puppet stuff. It had the weight of what she would have been, around eighty pounds.

It had a fluid movement, like a marionette, that we partially released and puppeteered at the same time. When it crashed to its knees and fell over, it hit the ground in a kind of rag-doll position that would have been very hard for a real person to do."

Photo by John Bruno

Brian Sipe and Arjen Tuiten apply the appliances to Kristen Stewart.

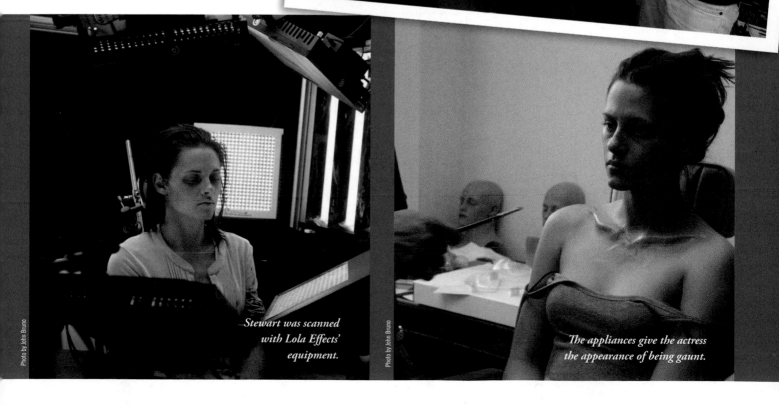

Photo by John Bruno

Stewart was scanned with Lola Effects' equipment.

Photo by John Bruno

The appliances give the actress the appearance of being gaunt.

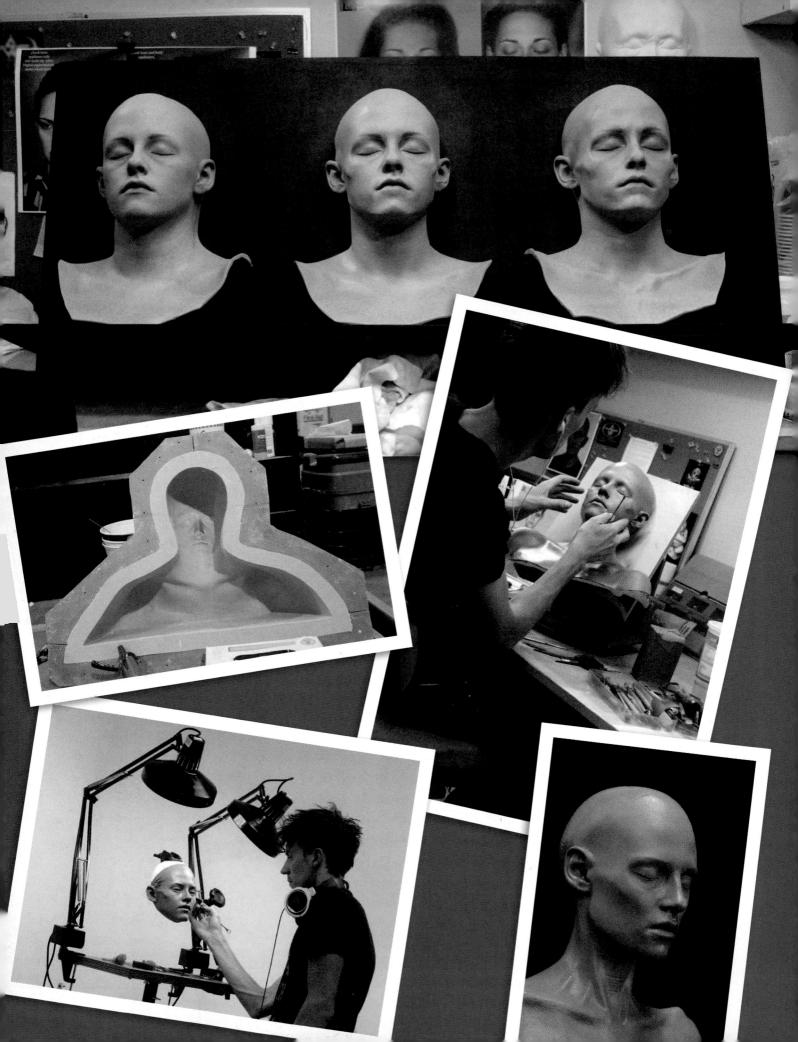

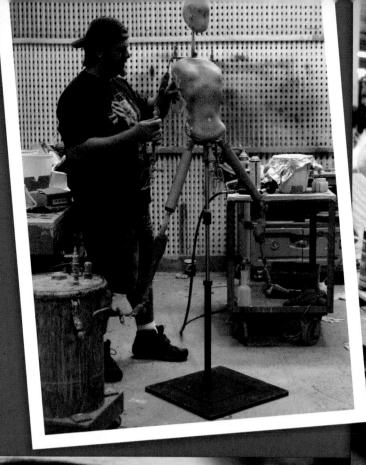

Legacy Effects went through many stages of sculpting and painting to create lifelike stand-ins for the dying Bella.

The birth itself takes place in Carlisle's study. The preproduction plans for modifications of the Cullen house had taken into account that the main area of the house, the second floor, was above the ground floor and Carlisle's study. "Bill wanted to have certain camera angles and luxuries to create the wonder of the infant's delivery," Bannerman said. "We had to put the camera in the ceiling to look straight down on Bella on the operating table, to understand her isolation and the severity of her physical condition."

"During the design process we built an eight-foot-by-eleven-foot removable panel in the ceiling," art director Flemming explained. "The ceiling piece was removed from above by chain motors attached to the grid. Then a camera crane was hoisted up onto the upstairs deck and we shot from above. Where there's a will, there's a way!"

As with Alice's bedroom, Carlisle's study was another never-before-seen room of the expansive house that gestated through Richard Sherman's art department, its look determined by the house itself. "Remember, the house is glass and wood and extremely modern," set decorator Schlesinger noted. "That drove a lot of our thinking. We went for a very clean, modern feel. The conference table we designed and built was a raw steel frame with a limestone insert, another very modern take on a classic shape. His desk was wooden, with a steel top reminiscent of the conference table, because they were in the same room."

For the transformation of the study into a delivery room, the set-decorating department brought in real medical equipment, including an anesthesia machine and the latest high-tech operating table. "Carlisle has that caretaker, small-town doctor feel," Flemming said, "but he's also a powerful and ancient vampire. He would get the most powerful equipment he could to deliver Bella's baby. That's how I approached it."

For the special operating table, the production secured two of the only four currently existing in the world. "This was a new, state-of-the-art operating table, the latest and greatest," Schlesinger said. "It has the ability to perform any procedure; it's incredibly adjustable. We got it through a medical [company] out of Atlanta."

What Rosengrant called another "old-school effect" portrayed Bella as she lay in labor on the operating table. Legacy built a whole lower torso that included the pregnant belly and skinny, emaciated legs, along with a duplicate of the operating table with a hole in its center. "We completed the replica table with machined-in steel and aluminium connection points that allowed us to use the real table's headrest and leg-support sections, to clip them into place on our table. Kristen came through the center portion of our table, and then we put the emaciated partial animatronic puppet version up against her. The fake legs were subtly puppeteered. I have to say, Kristen's performance brought to life the pain and agony of the birth."

"It's hard to describe, but I think for Kristen to get into the most vulnerable place means beating herself up, in some way, psychologically," Condon opined. "During the birth scene she stayed in the gurney [during breaks]. She just let everything happen around her. I thought that was interesting, and made total sense."

"Regardless of the prosthetics and visual effects, what really made the scene believable and emotional was that Kristen went to incredible places as an actress. There's this strength—she doesn't want to give up, she wants to make sure the child comes out alive before she gives up her life. It's a really intense, exciting part of the movie, with Rob and Taylor being there for her and trying to help her through it."

—WYCK GODFREY,
PRODUCER

Stewart gets made up on set for the birth scene.

The puppet created to stand in for the gaunt Bella.

Forest Fight

From left: Tyson Houseman as Quil, Kiowa Gordon as Embry, Bronson Pelletier as Jared, and Alex Meraz as Paul.

> *"The location was in the forest, by a river, and beautiful in the night."*
>
> —PENG ZHANG, CO-FIGHT COORDINATOR

A child is born, and new mother Bella has seemingly died giving life. But there is no time for tears—Sam and his wolf pack are on the way. "You can set up a majestic aerial scene romanticizing the wolves, but the sequence where the wolves are charging to the Cullen house to attack the baby justified a completely different approach when I was shooting the plates used by the visual effects guys and the Tippett company," Bannerman explained. "I integrated dynamic elements to convey the threat, with fast-moving landscapes and an open, rocky area, where you could see wolves jumping. A fast-moving camera is a level of the film language that augments the peril, raises the stakes, ramps things up a notch."

In the film, Carlisle, Esme, and Emmett take a chance to go and feed, leaving Edward, Jacob, Alice, and Jasper standing guard against the expected attack of the wolves. That night, out of the forest, they appear, and the battle begins at the back of the Cullen house. At a crucial point, Carlisle and the others return—"like the cavalry," Ken Kokka said.

The drama of the fight included a story point that increased the threat from the attacking wolves. "Bill Condon wanted to make sure Jasper, Alice, and Edward are weak, because they haven't fed in a while," Leven added. "Then, when Emmett, Esme, and Carlisle come back, they can do huge power moves the other three can't. So, during the first part of the battle, the Cullens are weakened and have to fight defensively. When the other three arrive, they can fight more offensively."

For co–fight coordinator Peng Zhang, the battle was on a daunting schedule—eighty shots to get in only five nights. But after months of being inside a Baton Rouge soundstage, working on a major sequence for the second movie, he welcomed the chance to be outdoors. Zhang brought his own stuntwork experience, which included doubling for Jackie Chan in *Rush Hour 3*,

Jacob (Lautner) gets fierce.

Jacob finds himself fighting his former wolf pack to protect the Cullens and Bella.

and fight coordinating credits that included the recent *Kick-Ass*.

One of Zhang's challenges in designing the battle was that one group of combatants wasn't even there—not only would the wolves be created with CG, the fight team had to keep in mind their outsized dimensions while choreographing a dramatic but believable fight. "It's a fantasy movie, but difficult to choreograph," Zhang noted. "In *X-Men*, a character might fly, but the superpowers of a vampire aren't clear. A lot of moves also didn't fit into the action because of the size and speed of the wolves. So I started with Phil Tippett's team. Phil and I did pre-viz together of the live action and wolves."

"The fight is such a contained area, I wanted to make sure we had all kinds of stuff happening all the time and kept continuity," Eric Leven explained. "The pre-viz was a way to know if, say, Jasper was fighting Quil here, what was behind them? I worked on location with Peng, and he was fantastic. He knows a lot about visual effects, which is helpful. He would take our original designs and overhead views and come up with a twist. There was a shot where Jasper grabs Sam and is tackling him, but he said, 'What if Jasper does a backflip and grabs him with his legs?' I felt very collaborative with him."

Bill Condon shot the main-unit "bookends," Tippett noted, with second-unit director Foerster focusing on the meat of the fight. Stunt coordinator Scott Ateah's team executed the wirework and stunt moves Zhang designed. The Tippett team also developed

*Edward stands in
the woods outside the
Cullen house.*

an animatic that provided a bird's-eye view, a rough battle plan to identify who was where at any given moment. Animatics were ultimately produced to convey the information for each shot. Shots were labeled—"Paul Bites Jasper" was one—and designed so thumbnails of the low-res wolves could be dropped into the live-action footage to clarify the action, while the low-res 3-D figures themselves were color coded to identify specific characters. It was a lot of simultaneous back-and-forth, Tippett film editor Mike Cavanaugh recalled: "We sent them the [overhead] pre-viz of the fight scene. Eric would show that to Peng, and the stunt guys would film some shots and their stuff would start getting cut into our cut."

"The stunt guys were very specific about

what they could do," Kokka added. "They shot stuff to give to Eric, and he cut that into the animatic and showed that to Bill. Some of that we put into our animatic; in other cases we left the stunt footage."

Stunt coordinator Scott Ateah, a thirty-year stunt veteran, estimated that ninety-five percent of the fight was accomplished in the planning stage. "The Wolf People, Tippett and his company, came up with their version of the wolf fight, we came up with our version, and over the course of a few weeks they got melded into one. At the rehearsal stage we set up in Vancouver, we put together a sequence with wires and cables and then filmed it, and Peng edited it together. Peng's choreography put the emphasis on drama and concern for the characters. Unless there's emotional involvement in a fight scene, it's just physicality. We wanted to put people in peril and make sure the emotional side was in there.

"Ultimately, we try to get into the director's head and give him *his* fight scene," Ateah added. "My job as stunt coordinator is to assist the director in achieving what's in his head. If he's not an action director, there's a seed growing there, and I have to figure out how to nourish that. On Bill's side it was a lot of showing [and saying], 'What do you think of this?' In the end we had an animatic of the fight sequence that was part animatic, part storyboard, part what we shot digitally in our rehearsal space. It was a long, arduous affair to narrow it all down. Even when we began filming, we were tweaking until everyone was happy with it."

The setup for the fight included figuring out where the stunt coordinator needed to set up the wire system to "fly" the actors and their stand-ins. "We had a truss that was, basically, like a snorkel," Ateah explained. "It was attached to a crane we could snake out into the trees,

> ## "They never do anything a physical wolf can't do; they just do it bigger, stronger, faster."

and had a physical pick for a cable that could go forty to fifty feet from the base of the crane. I had five different crews of scalers and riggers working. The scalers might put spikes on and climb the trees, like a linesman climbing a telephone pole. Other places we got in with mechanical lifts."

The choreography of the main actors and stunt performers on location included wolf references, from life-size and lightweight "standees" to a big green wolf head or the big, lumpy prop nicknamed "the potato." A double-duty Tippett crew moved the stand-ins around, and also collected the requisite surveying information and camera data vital to creating their shots.

A "gag" could be as simple as a stuntperson leaping off a ladder. To be flown or pulled, a "full jerk vest" provided structural support— the vest came over the shoulders and wrapped around the torso and under the legs; it could be cinched tight, with pick points through the stitched webbing. The "Hong Kong harness" went around the waist and legs, and was mostly used for quick jumps and landings.

"I was there with Bill, shooting the beginning of the fight, while Phil was off doing second-unit stuff. Bill is great with actors. He never just sat behind 'Video Village' [where directors watch monitors of the filming in progress] and shouted out orders. He would get up and go talk with the actors. He would take an actor aside, where no one else could hear, and quietly give them direction."

—ERIC LEVEN, VISUAL EFFECTS SUPERVISOR, TIPPETT STUDIO

Despite being supernatural characters, both the vampires and the wolves were grounded in physics, Ateah explained. "With the Tippett wolves, they never do anything a physical wolf can't do; they just do it bigger, stronger, faster—and then some. Same with the Cullens; they don't defy gravity. And each vampire has a specific skill. For example, Alice is like a gymnast who can fly through the air and do somersaults. Emmett is a big strong guy, like a football player, so he does a lot of shouldering and throwing. Each character had their own special flavor, but we always brought them together as a unit. Emmett might be smashing and crashing, but he'd get into trouble. Alice would save him, so the situation of Emmett's strength brings out Alice's athleticism. The important thing was to create drama by taking advantage of each character's strengths and weaknesses, keeping a flow going, like a dance, and involving everyone in the drama of it."

In his choreography, Zhang noted that his own stunt experience helped him gauge which parts of a sequence could be handled by the actors and which should be done by trained stuntpeople. "Robert did ninety percent of the fight himself, which was good, because you want to see the actor's face in there. He didn't have to fly on wires; he was all on the ground."

The production was worried the fight team wouldn't make their shots—originally, the fight had been planned for seven days, but that was whittled down to five. But Zhang's team did twenty setups a night, the fight coordinator

Booboo Stewart as Seth and Julia Jones as Leah Clearwater.

estimated, and easily made their shots in the days allotted. "We were really prepared—we had done so many tests to figure things out, and planned so well ahead of time," Zhang said. "The weather also helped us. It had been raining the whole time, but during the nights we were shooting it only rained about three hours."

As the ferocious fight between vampires and wolves reaches its height, Edward reads Jacob's thoughts and shouts for the fighting to stop. The wolves cannot kill one who has been imprinted—and Jacob has just imprinted with Bella's baby, the vampire/human child called Renesmee Carlie Cullen.

What is "imprinting"? As THE TWILIGHT SAGA: THE OFFICIAL ILLUSTRATED GUIDE explains, "Some werewolves experience a bonding inci-

dent called imprinting, in which they become unconditionally tied to a human of the opposite sex. . . . No matter the age or living conditions of the human, the werewolf automatically becomes whatever the human wants him to be, at the loss of his personal free will. If the human is young, the werewolf becomes the perfect platonic playmate and protector." In Meyer's mythology, it is against the law of the wolf pack to kill anyone a wolf has imprinted upon.[10]

"What is important for the audience to understand is that imprinting is not a romantic or sexual connection, but exists on a higher plane of consciousness," screenwriter Rosenberg explained. "This is important to understand when you have an adult imprinting on an infant. The trick was to keep the subject of imprinting

"JACOB'S ATTACHMENT TO BELLA IS ARCED AND RESOLVED IN HIS IMPRINTING ON RENESMEE."

it's the central external conflict in the first half of the book—but its resolution seemed to happen more behind-the-scenes," Rosenberg noted. "Since I was prominently playing that conflict, even escalating it, I wanted to let it manifest as a physical fight and play the climax and resolution of it on-screen. The entire movie builds to several events that occur at the end: Jacob's attachment to Bella is arced and resolved in his imprinting on Renesmee, Bella's arduous journey to becoming a vampire ends, and the wolf pack's conflict with Jacob reaches its height and is resolved. My goal was to maintain the urgency and the emotion right up to the end."

And, as always, the forest is where these primal and supernatural forces play out, adds cinematographer Guillermo Navarro. "The forest is there like a witness to this drama of the wolves attacking the Cullens, and all the interests between the wolves and vampires. It's where Jacob imprints upon Renesmee. The forest becomes this incredible protecting mother of all the community."

The fight crew finished its work at the end of April. By then the first unit had already wrapped principal photography in the Virgin Islands, where the production had gone to get the last shot that had eluded them in Brazil.

alive throughout the movie, and to explain it in spiritual terms, so that in the end, when Jacob imprints on Renesmee, the audience understands it as a spiritual connection."

The imprinting revelation helped tie up a number of narrative threads, including the key conflict from the novel that had been expanded upon in the film. "The split between Jacob and the wolves was very significant in the book—

Rosalie (Nikki Reed) holding Renesmee,
just before Jacob imprints.

Quil (Tyson Houseman) has
imprinted on Claire (Sienna Joseph).

Breaking Dawn

"I promised we would *try*," he whispered, suddenly tense. "If . . . if I do something wrong, if I hurt you, you must tell me at once."

. . . "Don't be afraid," I murmured. "We belong together."

I was abruptly overwhelmed by the truth of my own words. This moment was so perfect, so right, there was no way to doubt it.

His arms wrapped around me, holding me against him . . . It felt like every nerve ending in my body was a live wire.

"Forever," he agreed, and then pulled us gently into deeper water.

—BELLA AND EDWARD ARE FINALLY TOGETHER IN BREAKING DAWN. THIS WAS THE LAST SCENE ADAPTED AND FILMED IN PRINCIPAL PHOTOGRAPHY FOR *THE TWILIGHT SAGA* FILM FRANCHISE.[11]

The Twilight Saga films began in March 2008, with director Catherine Hardwicke leading a forty-five-day schedule of principal photography on the first adaptation. Principal photography for not only two *Breaking Dawn* films but the entire franchise wrapped on April 22, 2011.

The irony was that although the actors' work was completed, the series would not truly conclude until the second movie's release in November 2012. But anticipation remains high. "The films in the franchise have captured the attention of audiences around the globe," said Patrick Wachsberger, co-chairman and president of Summit Entertainment. "We believe that the last two films will be no different. While the story may have started in North America, the films continue to resonate in all parts of the world due to the series' universal themes and the fantasy that the film presents." Each film in the series had its theme, and the first *Breaking Dawn* would

be dramatically different from the final chapter. "*New Moon* was driven by romance, *Eclipse* was driven by menace and violence," Bill Bannerman concluded. "*Breaking Dawn Part 1* is very romantic and the launching point to set up the scope of *Part 2*."

In postproduction the film was edited into its final form, but Virginia Katz had been living with the footage since the first frame was shot. "In editing the main characters, the intention of the scene determined how I would cut it," Katz explained. "For example, if Jacob was with his human pack, the rhythm was snappier and faster than scenes with Bella that were more emotional. I loved cutting scenes between Edward and Bella because there is a tension that is palpable, a longing that permeates the screen. With Bella and Jacob, there is a different tension, a bittersweet and unattainable one. In the wedding, I knew it was important to be in Bella's head, to feel her anticipation. She was about to not only get married, but also to leave her old life behind.

"The honeymoon was a combination of rhythms. Bella's anxiety was fast-paced and fun. It was about her nervousness. When she gives in to that, the editing becomes more languid and sensual. In Bella's pregnancy, the editing is more fractured. Bella, Edward, and Jacob are all fighting their own emotional demons, and the challenge was to keep each story alive, yet cohesive. As Bella moved in and out of consciousness the cutting got more frantic.

"It's all about emotion, and how the characters feel."

During filming of *The Twilight Saga: Breaking Dawn* there had been the usual Twi-fan frenzy in Rio, and the helicopter that buzzed the filming of the wedding, but the work had been relaxed and professional during the long stretch of stage work in Louisiana. "What was fantastic was that, for some reason, they leave you alone down there," Godfrey said. "There were no paparazzi, or people waiting outside the actors' apartments. They had a real life."

The dual production was bookended with

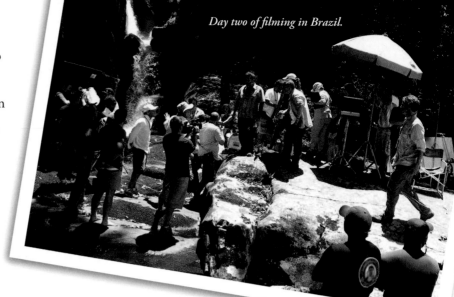

Day two of filming in Brazil.

> "AS BELLA MOVED IN AND OUT OF CONSCIOUSNESS THE CUTTING GOT MORE FRANTIC."

bad weather, from the storm that hit the first unit in Brazil to torrential rain and cold that made the wedding reception a less-than-joyous affair for cast and crew.

"Oh, boy!" Wilkinson sighed, recalling the rains that hit the reception. "We'd all filmed in Vancouver before, so we knew what we were up for. We were shooting this quintessential summertime wedding in the rainy season. The weather was cold and rotten, but the background actors really did well staying in good humor. We had a small army of costumers standing by with warm blankets. We had the women take off their strappy high heels to put on their warming boots."

"It was fun to work to release these films, and it should be a wonderful surprise and voyage of discovery for the audience. That's why we were always at pains to try to keep things [secret]. You wouldn't want to open your presents before Christmas Day! That's how we felt about the images we were creating."

—MICHAEL WILKINSON, COSTUME DESIGNER

> "I feel that for every great concept that's existed on film, casting is everything. The *Twilight Saga* films are perfectly cast the way *Star Wars* and *Raiders of the Lost Ark* are perfectly cast. These actors have charisma, and they look their parts. That's one of the reasons I wanted to be involved. This is one of those special projects."
>
> —JOHN BRUNO, VISUAL EFFECTS SUPERVISOR

And then there was the wedding dress. "Well, you can imagine the intensity surrounding this precious wedding dress," Wilkinson added. "We were lucky to have multiples, so we were constantly flip-flopping between them because for the majority of scenes, Kristen was walking on a surface that was wet and spongy. You know those TV commercials with the paper towels soaking up water? That was basically what her beautiful, floor-length dress with a four-foot train was doing. But all hats off to Kristen, for dealing with all those circumstances. She's the most patient, hardworking, and impressive young lady."

Guillermo Navarro also saluted Stewart. "Her character went through so many changes, and we were able to not only control her look, but make her look believable and really bad when she needed to look bad. We reached a level of control of the space she would be in, to light her in a way that was best for her."

"WE HAD A SMALL ARMY OF COSTUMERS STANDING BY WITH WARM BLANKETS."

"What can I say but 'Rain, rain, go away'?" hairstylist Rita Parillo reflected. "There are only a few things you can do with hair in the rain and, for the most part, they require help from other departments. First, if a hairstyle for a scene had not been established, we'd do a simple style that wouldn't require much maintenance. We would ask the locations department for a tent, not only as a spot to get in out of the rain, but a complete setup with a table, mirror, and electricity to touch up and maintain hair throughout the day. We also had PAs [production assistants] carry umbrellas to help cover an actor until the camera was ready to shoot. Let's face it—hair and water is not a good mix when trying to duplicate work for continuity."

Godfrey thought back to the early days of preproduction, when the scouting team stood in the middle of the forest and imagined what was to be built, and everything that might happen there. "At the time we were standing in the woods, there wasn't even a house there. We decided to do the reception outside." On the rainy filming days there was no choice: "We just had to go for it," Godfrey said.

Despite the rain during the filming of the reception, the sun came out for Bella and Edward's wedding. Among the guests were two notable couples—or, rather, four filmmakers playing couples. Melissa Rosenberg partnered with Bill Bannerman, while Stephenie Meyer came with Wyck Godfrey. They arrived with backstories, Rosenberg recalled. "Bill was a chiropractor and I was an interior designer who

Carlisle's note to the Volturi, informing them of Bella's transformation.

had redone his office. Wyck and Stephenie were locals, with Wyck one of the deputies who had worked with Charlie, and they decided they were having marital problems. It was all done for fun."

Rosenberg noted that the wedding ceremony kept getting pushed back because of weather concerns. "Then the production caught a window of sunlight and I jumped on a plane. Bill Condon put us in the last row, so when Bella came in and everyone rose to face her, we were right in front. It was cold, but physical discomfort aside, it was gorgeous. Our production designer did an extraordinary job. Kristen's dress was phenomenal—a great deal of attention went into designing that. After all these years of

following these characters, it was lovely to be able to say goodbye in this way."

It was quite a moment for Stephenie Meyer when Kristen Stewart's Bella began walking down the aisle, Bannerman recalled. "When the creator and her hero character joined eyes, it put closure to a very long journey they've both taken. It was a pretty emotional moment."

"The filmmaking, artistry, and commitment to Stephenie's work that have gone into the past three films continues with the last two installments in the franchise," said Rob Friedman, co-chairman and CEO of Summit Entertainment. "Bill Condon and his team give fans what they love from the last book, as well as their

"There's this amazing idea in vampire mythology that you get to live forever, but you pay a terrible price for it. What's interesting is the vampires we spend time with get to live forever, they don't kill people, they find true love, and they even have the next generation, they have children. They really do get to have it all! Immortality without a price."

—BILL CONDON, DIRECTOR

own personal connection to the material. For us this mix is truly inspiring and is a credit to the characters that Stephenie has created and the on-screen characters that our actors have helped to shape."

With the wedding and reception completed, hundreds of days of principal photography over five *Twilight Saga* films had come down to one final day. "Because of the storm in Brazil, we weren't able to shoot the night exterior ocean scene where Bella and Edward first make love," Godfrey explained. "We left Brazil knowing we'd have to find a place to shoot that scene. We shot our last night of the entire franchise in St. Thomas, U.S. Virgin Islands, on Good Friday of the Easter weekend.

"I've never been involved in a production that wasn't tinged with either 'Thank God *that's* over' or the bittersweet feeling of not wanting it to end. On this one there was a celebratory feeling: 'We did it!' And it was hard not to feel great on that last day in St. Thomas. The final scene was the first time Bella makes love. It wasn't pressure filled; everyone was happy and relaxed, jumping in the water and swimming. It was great, it was all meant to be.

"We shot all night; we worked till dawn. When we wrapped, it was still dark. And as we drove back to the hotel, the sun was coming up over the Caribbean Sea. It was like, 'Oh, wow—there it is. It's breaking dawn.'"

Aro (Michael Sheen) will be back in Part 2.

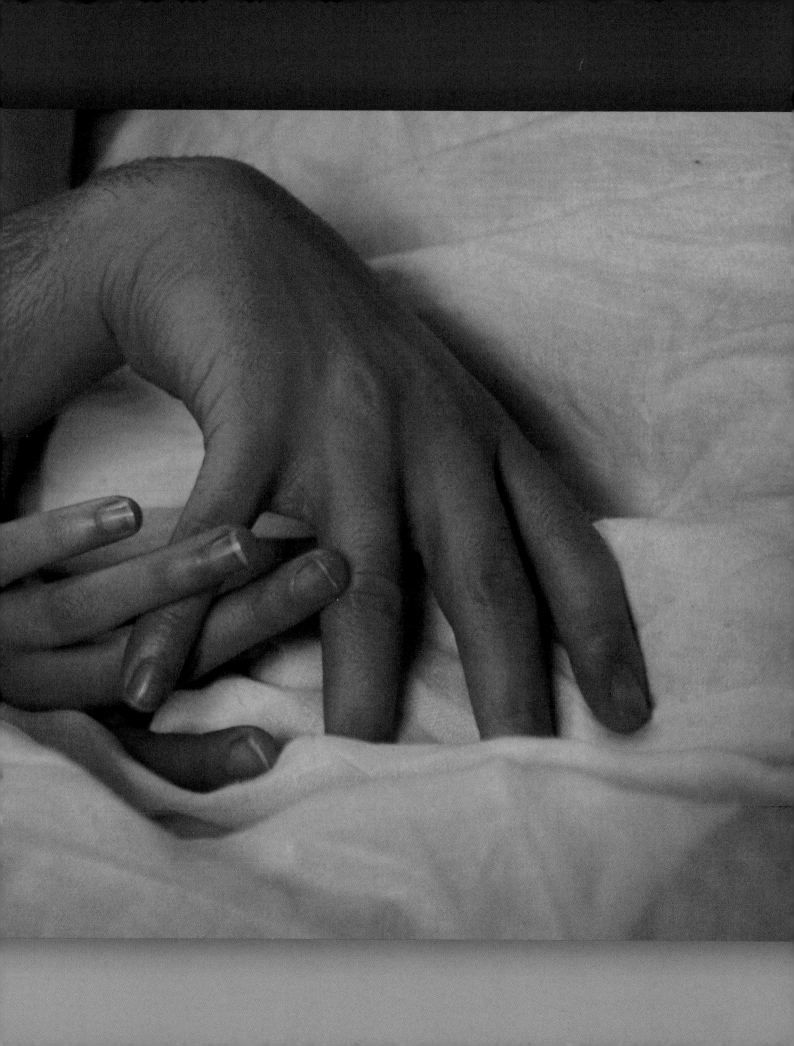

Notes

1: Stephenie Meyer, *Breaking Dawn* (New York: Megan Tingley Books, Little, Brown and Company, 2008), p. 22.

2: Stephenie Meyer, *Twilight* (New York: Megan Tingley Books, Little, Brown and Company, first paperback edition, 2006), p. 24.

3: Mark Cotta Vaz, *Twilight: The Complete Illustrated Movie Companion* (New York: Little, Brown and Company, 2008), p. 16.

4: Ibid., p. 20.

5: The cumulative worldwide box office, from the Box Office Mojo website, stands at $1,900,935,434. The breakdown for each film's worldwide grosses: *Twilight* (2008): $392,616,625; *The Twilight Saga: New Moon* (2009): $709,827,462; *The Twilight Saga: Eclipse* (2010): $698,491,347.

6: Jody Duncan, "Dark Phoenix Rising," *Cinefex* #106, July 2006: p. 39.

7: Vaz, *The Twilight Saga: Eclipse: The Official Illustrated Movie Companion,* pp. 42–43.

8: Meyer, *Breaking Dawn*, pp. 23–24.

9: Rosengrant runs Legacy with Stan Winston Studio veterans Shane Mahan, Lindsay MacGowan, and Alan Scott.

10: Stephenie Meyer, *The Twilight Saga: The Official Illustrated Guide* (New York: Megan Tingley Books, Little, Brown and Company, 2011), pp. 310–311.

11: Meyer, *Breaking Dawn*, p. 84.

A great resource during the preparation of this book was Stephenie Meyer's *The Twilight Saga: The Official Illustrated Guide* (New York: Megan Tingley Books, Little, Brown and Company, 2011).

Special thanks to Lori Petrini, John Bruno, and Cole Taylor for additional images.

Acknowledgments

I'm grateful to Little, Brown and Company for asking me to chronicle this latest chapter of *The Twilight Saga*. Editor Erin Stein once again made it all come together, and beautifully so. Jennifer Smuckler, executive assistant to Nancy Kirkpatrick at Summit Entertainment, was invaluable in helping connect me with the filmmakers. And a tip of the hat to all who helped along the way, including Greg Yolen, assistant to Bill Condon, and Lori Petrini at Tippett Studio. I also salute the filmmakers, many of whom were under the gun of *Breaking Dawn* deadlines when they graciously took time to share their thoughts.

I have to give a shout-out to my family for all their loving support, and to my loving sweetheart, Edris. I'm also enriched by the friendship and hard work of my agent, John Silbersack, and his stellar assistant, Nicole Robson.

And to Mike Wigner, World's Greatest Bike Messenger: Wig, it's a wrap—see you at Vesuvio's.

Author's Credits

Mark Cotta Vaz is the author of the previous titles in the #1 *New York Times* bestselling The Twilight Saga movie companion series. His books on film include *Industrial Light + Magic: Into the Digital Realm*, a history of the second decade of George Lucas's famed visual effects house; the award-winning *The Invisible Art: The Legends of Movie Matte Painting*, co-authored with Academy Governor and Oscar® winner Craig Barron; and the critically acclaimed *Living Dangerously: The Adventures of Merian C. Cooper*, creator of King Kong. This movie companion is Vaz's thirtieth published book.

Go Behind the Scenes of Your Favorite Movies...

Get an insider's look at the making of *Twilight*, *New Moon*, and *Eclipse* with the only **official** movie companions! They feature exclusive images and interviews with production designers, makeup artists, hairstylists, producers, and more. You'll see firsthand how your favorite books became blockbuster movies.

LITTLE, BROWN AND COMPANY

Available now wherever books are sold.

The #1 Bestselling Books
That Started It All

And don't miss . . .

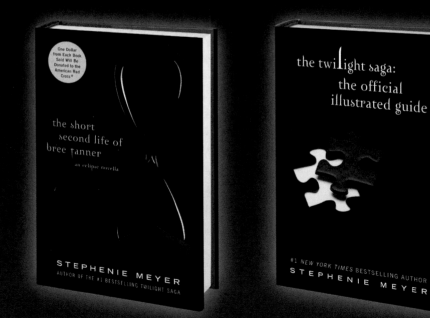

www.TheTwilightSaga.com